I0619734

Copyright © 2021 by Camille Douglass
All rights reserved.
Cursed Spirits
First Publication: February 2021
Dead Mouse on Cheese Publishing
ISBN: 978-1-950163-06-9 (ebook)
ISBN: 978-1-950163-07-6 (paperback)

Cover Art: Deranged Doctor Design

For my dad, a.k.a. the only person who has ever snuck a Jell-o shot out of a bar to bring home to me

ACKNOWLEDGMENTS

This past year has tested everyone I know, including myself. I couldn't have finished this book without the endless support I've had from my family and friends. Thank you to my mom, dad, Danielle, D.J., Ida, Alicia, and Jami. You all kept me sane through a pandemic, work stress, a broken leg (in addition to two sprained ankles), and the million other things 2020 threw at us. I'm sure I missed a few of you but if you've seen me on a Zoom call or any other video call app this year, know that you're important to me.

Deranged Doctor Design, you always deliver amazing covers. Finally, to the readers, I hope you enjoyed Peg's latest adventure.

A PEG DARROW NOVEL

CURSED SPIRITS

CAMILLE DOUGLASS

1

The last time I'd seen Deval, I'd slammed a door in his face. The time before that, I'd been panicked to the point of hysteria and fled from a full restaurant on Valentine's Day, as ghosts swarmed around me. I still cringed when I remembered that night.

Now, I stood over my inflatable aboveground pool. A little present I'd bought myself to help me deal with my new reality. When I floated in water with my ears submerged, I couldn't hear what the spirits were going on about. I'd wanted a break from them this afternoon. In preparation I'd slathered my normally pale skin, now turned mildly golden, with a high SPF and thrown on an old black bikini. Sadly, one of the few joys left in my world had been tainted. A dead goblin floated in the pool, head and body detached, from one another bobbing like a macabre Halloween display.

Cheddar, my moderately tubby feline companion, sat next to me and meowed mournfully.

"You just want to use the pool as a scratch pad. I actually have real problems."

He meowed again.

"I know that it's the small things, Cheddar, but by scratching the pool you'd be destroying one of my small things. I didn't think you were that petty."

I looked down at him, and he twitched his tail at me, telling me plainly that he was that petty. I sighed and grabbed my phone from a patio table I'd dragged next to the pool. The fuzzy imprint of a robust woman hissed at me as I reached through her. I looked at her a little dead-eyed and shrugged.

"I've gotta live my life, Judith."

She hissed again but turned her back to me and moved away in a motion that could be described as equal parts floating and staggering. A neat trick.

I shook my head and leaned over the pool edge to get a better look. The clear water had a tinge of pink that would indicate blood, but not enough to suggest that he'd been killed in my yard. It was not as though a goblin would stop by my place for a late-night swim even if the very apparent cause of death hadn't been a factor.

An aboveground pool meant cheap trash by Arizona standards. As the proud owner of one, I still found them delightful, but since every third house sported an in-ground number that cost significantly more than the two-fifty I'd spent at one of the big box stores, I doubted the man's killers had come across my yard at random. Especially given that the man lacked clothing.

I looked down at my cat again, "You know what this means."

He meowed mournfully.

"I need to call the goblins."

He stared at me without blinking.

"Look, Cheddar, I like Deval, too. I'm the one who is

2

supposed to be his magical soul mate. Guess what? The world isn't all sunshine and soul mates."

He just kept staring at me.

"Okay, fine. It's June in the desert; it is all sunshine, but not all soul mates. And, I'd appreciate it if you didn't make my personal sacrifice feel worse than it already does."

Cheddar turned around and started to groom himself with one of his back feet in the air in a move that my friends and I labeled "playing the cello." I turned to give him a little privacy and then looked down at my phone. I hesitated for a split second and then selected the entry I had for Queen Delmy, who ruled the Southwest goblins.

The call rang on for what felt like minutes before a robot voice listed off the number I'd just called. I hung up before the beep could sound in my ear. Being ninety percent sure that a number still belonged to the queen of the goblins was not one hundred, and I didn't want to talk about dead goblins on the voicemail of some rando. That meant only one thing. I looked at my phone contacts and swallowed. I scrolled to his contact info and pressed enter. Despite my prayers to the gods that he send me to voicemail, he answered on the third ring.

"Ms. Darrow." His tone was cold, impersonal.

I bit the inside of my own cheek in self-punishment. "Deval, I have one of your people."

A moment of silence passed. "What do you mean, you have one of my people?"

"I mean he's in my pool." Ugh, what was wrong with me? "Dead, there's a dead goblin in my pool."

Another pause. "Did you kill him?"

"No, I came out here to float, and there's a naked, decapitated goblin in my pool."

"Are you acquainted with this goblin?" He asked, his tone still frustratingly neutral.

"No, Deval, I do not know the naked man in my pool."

"How long has he been there?"

I looked at my phone again. It read ten o'clock in the morning. "He wasn't here at midnight last night when I was in the pool."

"When did you have a pool installed?" He calmly inquired.

"I removed an aboveground pool from a box and installed it with an air pump mid-May. Any other questions, or could you just send your people out here. I'm trying to enjoy my summer." The ghosts had begun to gather, but they kept their distance for the moment as I eyed them warily.

"Surviving a desert summer is enjoyment enough," Deval responded, deadpan.

Sweat began to form on my chest and work itself down my cleavage in an uncomfortably sticky way. The only rational reason to be outdoors in Arizona in the month of June was to be in a lukewarm pool, but there was no way I'd get in now.

"When are your people coming?"

"I can be there within the hour."

"I don't know if that's a good idea, Deval."

"What, because you chose to end our relationship abruptly?"

I had no response to that, so I gritted my teeth.

Deval let the silence linger a beat before continuing. "I will be along with Griselda. Please do not touch the body; I am currently undecided if your services as a fortune will be necessary," he said referencing my job as a Soldier of Fortune for the Arizona witches.

I ended the call, walked over to a patio chair, and sank into it. I almost instantly realized my mistake. I'd been distracted by Deval and allowed too many specters to gather near me. The ghosts realized that I didn't have a quick escape and swarmed around me. They pressed in more closely. Goosebumps raised on my inadequately covered body. Too many voices to distinguish assaulted me to the point that they became one deafening hum.

I tried to stand up and even mentally reached for the door to my plane "George," but I had waited too long, and I fell back into my seat as the trance began. I'd seen this happen to Alice. Her eyes would turn pale and lifeless as she stared into space. I hadn't understood it then. I did now. I let go and fell into the void with the spirits.

That was how I found myself shivering in an old black bikini on a hundred-degree day with a goblin prince kneeling before me. He'd placed his hands on my knees and the warmth from him felt like fire on my ice-cold skin, jolting me back to the here a now. Goblin temperatures usually ran low, so the heat coming from him was a strong indicator that I'd gone too far into the abyss. The swarm of spirits had backed off, but my mind was still abuzz with all their auras clinging to me. It took a moment to realize that Deval was speaking to me.

I shook my head again, attempting to clear my mind and my vision. I could make out his features clearly and another person stood several feet behind him, but my vision stayed stubbornly fuzzy. I really needed to get in the shower. Water cleared energies and restored me when I had had an episode. I'd found that tidbit in one of Alice's personal diaries after her death, but I'd already suspected it from my own addiction to taking constant baths and showers. Still, I could see his mouth moving but he sounded, like the teacher from the old *Peanuts* cartoons, warbled beyond comprehension.

"Deval, I can't understand you or see very well at the moment. Would you be so kind as to lead me to my shower?" I could have made it myself and had in the past, but I really didn't want an audience if I ran into walls and furniture along the way. He stood and grabbed my elbow, marching me through my own home before unceremoniously lifting and setting me in the bathtub.

I heard the metal scratch of the shower rings dragged along the rod and a thump of the door closing. These sounds had been clear despite my foggy brain. That meant I was coming back. I fumbled with bathtub knobs, briefly scalding myself before hitting the right adjustment and pulled up on the shower spigot. The slightly cool-to-warm water rushed over me. My vision righted itself, and I could now make out Deval whispering to someone I assumed to be Griselda in my hallway.

I took a deep breath and allowed myself one moment of peace, leaning my forehead against the cool tiles that lined my shower, but only for a moment before I straightened and turned off the water. Stepping onto the bathmat, I grabbed a towel and started rubbed at my limbs and torso vigorously since a chill still lingered on my skin. Being found comatose in a bikini wasn't great unless, of course, you needed to be put in a shower by your guests. Then it was just convenient.

The other unlikely convenience was the heavy purple bathrobe that sat on a hook on the back of my bathroom door. It had been an impulse purchase, and I'd come to find I wasn't a robe person. Either the weather was too warm to justify the heavy garment, or it was chilly and I wanted to jump straight into my clothes. Right now, I was just grateful that I didn't need to exit the room still clad in a bikini. I slid the robe on and pulled it around myself, tying it when it was closed from my neck to past my knees, in what could only be described as matronly. With that, I took a deep breath and turned the knob.

He stood just outside the door by himself. He had been successful at shooing off Griselda.

"Uh, sorry about that," I stammered, "a spell from last night must have had some after effects," I lied.

He tilted his head giving me a hard stare and stepped forward grabbing my upper arm in a firm grip. "Do you think I do not know what that was? I am not some young fool who would not recognize the mantle you now carry. Why would you not tell me this?"

I yanked my arm out of his grip mildly panicked. The mantle he spoke of was the reason I couldn't see him anymore. The death reader mantle had been passed to me upon the murder of my friend Alice. It allowed me to see and speak to ghosts, but it also had many downsides one of which was that people would murder to gain the power. Only Pammy and Lola knew I carried it, and if I didn't want to be hunted, I needed to keep it that way. "I have no idea what you're talking about Deval." I attempted to walk past him.

He pivoted from the wall, now blocking me in my own damn hallway. "I was friends with Alice and many of her predecessors. I know the signs of the trance. Why would you not tell me?"

I attempted to turn around and head toward my bedroom, but he reached out grabbing my shoulder spinning me to face him. That was too far.

I shoved my finger into his chest. "Listen here, buddy, I don't know what it is you think you know but you're mistaken. I've said all I'm going to say about this."

He took another step forward, and it was just enough to

make my already frazzled magic go on the warpath. A tingling sensation burst to my palms. I looked down and saw that my normal green magic flaring to life but along with it came a new color. I'd been too recently in the void, and the purple light came out bright and clear along with the green. I looked up and met his eyes knowing mine had gone full goblin metal as well. It took every tiny ounce of willpower I had left, but I managed to pull it back in and not release the magic. When my palms no longer tingled and I felt my eyes shift to normal, I took a step back, giving myself a foot of personal space and bent forward setting my hands on my knees and taking a big breath. I straightened and stared back at Deval.

He searched my face. "This is why you left. Why you stopped seeing me. Who is sowing doubt in your mind that you thought you could not trust me?"

I wanted to say something, anything. He knew my truth. The last few months of excruciating self-doubt felt silly now. Not because I could be with him now. I didn't think that had changed, but because I thought that I could keep the mantle secret. I'd thought that Alice had been able to do so, but in retrospect how many had really known? Pammy for sure, probably Bruce, and now Deval. Had I been that foolish?

"Everything I've read, everything I've learned, those I've spoken with, living and dead, all say the same thing. This is a path best tread alone. Even the most well meaning of friends have the potential for treachery. There's not a way for me to pass it on without dying. For some reason beyond my knowledge, Alice thought that this was my destiny. Right now, Deval, I'm just trying to survive. I want to trust you, and if this hadn't happened, I'm sure that we could have had our heyday. Reality is that I no longer see romantic entanglements as a possible future for me. It would leave me vulnerable, and let's be honest, it will only be a matter of time before people start calling me an Almond Joy."

"Are you done with this nonsense?" Deval had folded his arms and stared at me through my ramble. "Half of what you have just repeated to me obviously came directly from some long dead person's diary, and why are you speaking of candy bars?"

"Uh, yeah, dude, I literally just said I had read it, and it's the candy bar with nuts. People are gonna call me nuts or batshit like they called Alice. I doubt the goblin queen wants a daughter-in-law who is considered insane. She's how many centuries old? She's probably never even heard of modern mental health. Fifty bucks says she'd lock me in the attic like some poor creature in a gothic novel." Okay, even I knew I'd been pushing it there, but half-a-dozen ghosts had decided to join us in the already claustrophobic hallway.

"My mother is, in fact, a fan of modern mental health and despite the modern conveniences and luxuries, we are able to create in our mountain homes, I do not believe I am aware of any attics."

The corner of my mouth twitched. I wanted to smile. To say, aw shucks, you're right, everything is fine now. Instead I looked warily beyond his shoulder at our new guests.

"They've returned?"

"They always do."

He went silent, and I figured that was the answer I needed until I felt it: the vibration in my feet was a strong steady buzz. What I imagined a small earthquake felt like. The already sheer spirits faded to nothing as the low hum worked itself up my body, and I could feel it in my clenched jaw. I looked back to Deval. His eyes shone with his magic.

"What did you just do?" I demanded.

"What I would have taught you months ago if you had simply told me. The spirits are tied to this earth for their own reasons. They do not like to feel untethered from it, and if you learn to utilize this, there is no reason to believe that insanity is your only future."

"It can't be that easy. Alice would have said something. After she died, in one of her letters, it stated that her family has held the mantle on and off for centuries. She would have known." My voice got louder with every word.

"That's just it, Peg; her family is a family of witches. Witches may have the most versatile magics, but they do not hold dominion over the earth like goblins do. I never told her of this because it was not something that would have helped her. To offer a solution that one cannot use would be cruel and unnecessary."

"How did you even know it was possible if the witches have held it for centuries?"

"They haven't always held it, as I'm sure you've figured out."

My mind felt like a million gears had snapped together in an instant and began to turn. The possibilities felt infinite, but it still felt too easy.

"Please wait outside, Deval. We need to talk, and I need to not be in a bikini while we do so, and there's still the matter of the dead goblin in my pool."

"There is that." He agreed before turning and walking out my back door.

2

I emerged from my home fifteen minutes later—mainly because I'd needed to sit on my bed for a few minutes to get caught up on my own thoughts. After assuming the self-imposed role of martyr over the last four months, it was strange to sit there and think that maybe my life could be normal after all. Not completely normal but at least not leaving me in a constant state of fear. I still hadn't really figured out what the point of being a death reader was. For the most part, I'd found the spirits to be invasive assholes who seemed to enjoy putting me into a trance at the most inconvenient of times. There were, of course, exceptions, but I hadn't signed up for this job, and once I had it, I really didn't see why anyone would want it despite everything I'd read to the contrary.

Outside, Deval and Griselda stood over my pool. Staring at the body.

"Do you know who it is?" I asked as I approached.

Griselda gave me a once over. We'd bonded on a case a few months ago, but the closed look she gave me now indicated that she probably didn't appreciate me leaving Deval in the lurch while I dealt with being driven mad by specters no longer of this world. I set my jaw. I couldn't take back what I'd done and frankly with the information I'd had at the time, I stood by my decision.

She gave me a small nod of acknowledgement before turning back to the body.

"It's Bill."

"Bill?" I asked a little nonplussed. Goblin mothers tended to name their kids with a bit more gravitas. Maybe it was short for something else.

"Just Bill. His family preferred simplicity. All the kids had one syllable names." Griselda picked up what I'd been laying down.

"You guys have any idea why he'd end up in my pool?"

"We are at war," Deval said, voice flat with him standing very still as he studied the body in the pool.

"What do you mean you're at war?" My stomach started to churn.

"The goblins are at war. My uncle and cousin went to Europe for reinforcements. They didn't get the backing they'd hoped for from the European families, but they did manage to hire a ruthless mercenary army. I'd considered sending someone to inform you, but I didn't think they would care to involve you. It appears I was mistaken."

"I don't understand. Why would they involve me, period?"

"You were there when Vegard was murdered, you carry goblin blood, you have been a love interest for me, or it could be any number of things. My guess would be mostly the latter. My cousin does enjoy stirring the pot."

"So, what does this mean for me?"

"It means, fortune, that people wish you dead. So business as usual for you. It also means that Bill here will not be going home tonight to his three children because some megalomaniac wanted to make a point to Deval, and he knew of just the place to drop the body." Griselda's voice was as hard as steel.

My face instantly heated at the accusation, but before I could react, Griselda had turned on her heel and exited through the side gate of my yard.

Deval remained silent next to me.

"I didn't mean to make it about me. I just don't understand why this happening."

He sighed. "This is the life you've had for over six months. Would you say that you regularly enjoy a peaceful existence?"

"I would say that dead bodies don't usually wind up in my yard. I've definitely had a goblin asshole break in to my home in the past, but I've taken care of that asshole."

He let the silence stretch for a beat before responding. "Yes, my actions may not have always been the wisest in the past. Perhaps I am being unfair, but many things are happening at the moment, and I need you to be the strongest version of yourself right now because I don't have time to coddle anyone. My people are being murdered and," he inclined his head toward me, "terrorized."

I wanted to be mad, I really did, but I was supposed to be the badass fortune, though even badasses liked to know what they were up against. I could, however, hear the exhaustion in his voice. I'd already run off Griselda, and frankly I'd had some pretty life-altering revelations happen to me as well as a spirit-induced trance in the last hour.

"What can I do to help?"

He turned to me, eyes searching my face. "Do you actually wish to help?"

"Of course, I want to help. I'm not a military strategist or anything. I probably wouldn't hurt anyone, but there's a chance I'll get tranced again and end up a shish kebab on one of those spiky poles."

"Spiky poles?" He turned toward me and I saw a twitch at the corner of his mouth.

"You know, the ones people charge on horses with."

"A lance? Why on earth would we resort to jousting?"

"I don't know. I was just saying I may not be the best in battle. You said European mercenary army and my mind goes to either jousts a la renaissance fairs or Vlad the Impaler. I didn't say it was logical, but that's not the point." I raised my hands in the universal gesture of "hell if I know" and shrugged.

"Fine, we will not request that you take the knight's oath or perform any jousts. What I do need from you, now that I know you carry the mantle, is spies."

Spies? "I'm also not that great at undercover work, Deval."

"Why do you think the death reader mantle is coveted?"

"People want to talk to their dead grandma? I honestly think that if I John Edward this shit I could make a fortune because I can actually talk to the dead."

"Whereas I do not think you need to be as cautious as you have been. Doing cold readings on national television is not what I had in mind. The spirits you converse with can go anywhere. I'd like you to ask some to start looking for the mercenaries."

I gave him a skeptical look. "Deval, I'm not exactly buddy-buddy with these people. Half the time they're trying to get me to do something malicious to someone who did them dirty in life, and the other half of the time I feel like they are deliberately attempting to send me to an asylum. I'm happy that you have some history with people who have carried this power before, but just because I can talk to them doesn't mean I can control them."

"It's not about control, Ms. Darrow. As you have said, these beings come to you and request things from you. You have not learned how to successfully work with them. Just like the living, they all have aspirations for something, or they would not linger. Find out what it is that they want and take advantage of that desire."

"Ever heard of mansplaining, Deval? Whereas, I appreciate your second-hand knowledge, I don't think you actually have a clue about interactions with the dead."

"Oh, but he does." The disembodied voice for Judith drifted from over my shoulder.

"Mind your own damn business," I said over my shoulder.

"Excuse me?"

"You know damn well I'm talking to a ghost," I snapped at Deval.

"I did not actually know that, but I suspected. Is this person around regularly? Have you created a connection to them where you could bargain for assistance?"

I looked over my shoulder and looked at Judith.

"You know what I want."

I turned back to Deval. "Yeah, no can doozeville. Judith would like me to drive to her ninety-six-year-old sister's ranch in Utah and burn down her barn. Preferably when her livestock are in it. If that's too much trouble given the distance, she'd also be willing to accept my poisoning her great-niece since she's local and to quote her 'the bitch really likes that one.'" I held up my hands and added air quotes.

Deval's brows furrowed. "What did her sister do?"

I couldn't quite remember off the top of my head. In

the beginning, I'd tried to listen to everyone, and now their stories got mixed in my head.

"Judith, did your sister steal your first husband or did she buy the champion barrel horse out from under you, and then go on to make a shit ton of money in prize money and stud fees?"

"Both."

I turned my attention back to Deval. "Apparently it was both. So, I'm not saying Judith's sister doesn't have something coming, but I'm not killing a bunch of animals or poisoning some twenty-year-old who probably doesn't even know that her doddering grandma was in a feud with her long-dead sister."

"I would not suggest doing either. Surely, she can be reasoned with?"

Judith hissed again.

I shook my head. "I think death may have made her just a tad feral."

"Okay, perhaps she is not one to be reasoned with."

Judith began to curse a blue streak behind me, but I tuned her out.

"Like I said, I haven't really had any great experiences yet. But—I will say that due to the whole swarming me thing, I've spent most of my time hiding from them in my plane or in the pool."

"They cannot reach you when you are in your George?" He asked referring to the sentient dimension that had bonded with me.

I nodded my head.

"Interesting. Do you think you'd be more willing to attempt negotiations now that you know you can force them to disperse?"

"Maybe. I can certainly look into it. Part of the problem is that I can't spend as much time as I want researching because if I spend too long at Alice's, they find me, and then I get stuck there."

"You are still able to access the library?"

"I have been." I said cautiously. I'd actually inherited the library and the responsibility of having to maintain it long term gave me hives, but I'd already been pretty loose lipped, and I began to worry that I'd been too willing to drop the secret with Deval.

"Are you the only one with access?"

"I really couldn't say." I mean technically, yes, because I owned the building, but I didn't know every witch that Alice had granted access to over the years, and with her gone and my continued inability to make her wards bend to my will beyond allowing me access, I would guess that anyone with the right password would be able to enter any time they pleased. This was one of the many reasons why I decided to stay in my own home.

"If I teach you the vibration, would you be willing to attempt to negotiate with some of the spirits a bit more docile than Judith?"

"If I say 'no,' does that mean you won't teach me the vibration?"

He scowled. "Of course, I still would. Do you believe me to be such a cad as to stand by and watch your mental faculties disappear?"

"No," I begrudgingly admitted. "I just wanted to make sure."

He rolled his eyes but reached out and grabbed both of my hands in his.

Before I could make a peep of protest, he lifted my hands up with his so they were just bent at the elbow and stepped out broadening his stance and bending his knees slightly. I mimicked the stance automatically, and he nodded in approval without uttering a sound.

He pulled my fists forward then and placed them, still balled, on his chest, and he began to hum something deep and rich from his torso. I could feel the corner in my psyche that connected me to George and him stir eagerly at the sensation. The bottoms of my feet tingled, and I had the strong urge to kick off my sandals and feel the earth directly beneath my skin. Instead, the sensation moved up through my body until I found myself harmonizing with Deval's deeper pitch.

After only thirty seconds, he released my hands and stepped away. I held the vibration on my own for an additional thirty seconds before he held up his hand for me to stop. I stopped, and the unexpected quiet was startling. I turned and looked around my yard. Normally even if they weren't near me, the spirits tended to linger on the outskirts of my vision. Nope, none, nada, zilch. They had all gone, and the sudden, overwhelming relief at not being watched and analyzed by strangers twenty-four-seven, *the freedom of it,* left my knees wobbly.

"Do you see any of them?"

I shook my head "no," but I continued to stare around my yard in wonder. You never knew the luxury of privacy until you no longer had it.

"I do not know how long it will last, but my mother told me the stories of the last goblin death reader. My mother said she would begin to go into a trance, and suddenly every living being in the room felt like they were standing on one of those joke handshake buzzers. It didn't last long, but she would perform the magic and come back out of her trance."

"That is amazing, Deval. You said you didn't tell Alice about it. Are you sure only goblins can do it?"

"We control the earth. Witches can mimic us, but they cannot send the vibration deep enough to make the dead feel untethered without causing a natural disaster. They do not possess the knowing of the earth to do so. That and even with the natural disaster option, it would take significant work and is not practical."

"Yeah, I would think that causing an earthquake every other day would be problematic," I said dryly. "I'm still surprised that I didn't find anything in her books or papers about it.

"Have you been able to read them all? Study them thoroughly? You said it was difficult to remain clear-headed in that space."

"Hmmm, well, I guess I'd better go take another look. Maybe try and find some ghosts who aren't quite as blood thirsty as the others to bargain with." I looked down at my feet a little overwhelmed with hope. Hope that I wouldn't lose my mind, hope that I could have a normal life, maybe even hope that Deval and I could start again the relationship that had barely begun. I looked up at him then. "I don't know how to thank you. I feel as though you have given me my life back."

Whatever he'd been expecting me to say, it wasn't that, and he looked startled. "I only wish you'd trusted me enough to speak of this with me sooner."

You and me both, Buddy.

3

On Deval's advice, I decided I should go and take another look at the diaries Alice had left behind. That and as the ghosts lingered there I decided it might be a good place to try and find some spectral spies. I just needed to gather them in a group, tell them not to get too close because I now had a zapping trick, and ask for volunteers who didn't want me to commit bodily harm to any living being to raise their hands. Probably easer said than done, but that was my plan. So, after some awkward small talk and the reappearance of Griselda with a few other lackeys to discreetly remove the body from my pool, I had left home.

Initially, I'd considered using the door I'd created from George to quickly pop over to Alice's former home-slash my recent inheritance and burden but decided against it. Guilt gnawed at me thinking of the library as such, but I pushed it back into the compartment where I kept other uncomfortable feelings. I replaced it with the joy I felt at being able to go out and about in public, which meant I could stop by a coffee shop on the way.

My caffeine detour took a little longer than I had planned, so when I finally arrived, I pulled up directly in front of the facade of Alice's ruin rather than park a couple blocks away as I usually did to assist with the appearance of abandonment. My mild recklessness had felt reasonable given my desire to not walk two blocks in hundred-degree weather. Unfortunately, when I pulled up, I found something I wasn't expecting.

Through my windshield, I spotted three women standing on the doorway to the Phoenix First Baptist Church. They were close enough to the door that the magical façade hiding the restored building behind its former dilapidated state would have dropped if they were witches. Even the fake version was stunning: white stucco with Italian Gothic architecture, a lone bell tower rose from what appeared to be fire-damaged building.

My hand lingered on the overly warm handle in my car, and I pulled back when the metal got too hot to hold. The women were looking every which way around the building, and I seriously considered just driving away. I didn't want to give a tour, shoo off any humans, or talk to anyone, period. Despite the dead body aspect of the morning, I'd also finally been allowed a bit of peace and quiet, and my sanity desperately needed a little me time. Suck it up, buttercup, I muttered internally and grabbed the handle allowing the slight burn as I opened the door.

I approached the building, and I saw the three women more clearly. There were two older women who were accompanied by a younger one. The two women in their fifties were dressed opposite of one another. One of the women wore one of those odd summer suits consisting of Capri dress pants and a short-sleeved jacket: the pattern was a beige fabric covered in palm fronds. She had artful makeup applied in a very classic, understated way except the frosted pink lipstick. Her hair was dyed and teased to look like a blonde football helmet a la *Steel Magnolias*. Unfortunately, the Phoenix heat is not kind to makeup, and I saw that she'd begun to take on a slightly melted look.

Her counterpart wore no makeup and her hair was pulled back in a graying French braid that was thicker than it had a right to be. This woman wore flip-flops, a tank top, and jean short cut-offs that showed off tan, strong legs that looked like they belonged on a woman half her age. The third person was in her teens, maybe early twenties, and was fairly non-descript. Light brown hair to her chin. Minimal make up, a pair of knee-length shorts that came off as matronly for someone her age to wear and a thin T-shirt.

"You, there!" French braid called out in a distinctly backwater drawl. "Do you know the password?"

I instantly regretted getting out of my car. I knew my passcode to enter via the front of the building; my personal entrance didn't require one since I came through the goblin plane. I was almost positive that the pass phrase Alice had given me long ago was exclusive to me because the magic had scanned me when I'd used it, but I wasn't one hundred percent sure and didn't want to share it with strangers.

"Ummm." I didn't know how to respond and stood rooted at the end of the sidewalk clutching my purse in one hand and the decidedly melted iced latte I'd grabbed at a drive-through in the other.

"Well, missy, do you know it or not?" She continued, obviously nonplussed by my discomfort.

"I don't feel comfortable letting people in who aren't keyed to the library." At this point I just assumed they were witches.

"Listen here." Pants suit joined the conversation. She too had a drawl but a decidedly more sophisticated one. I could picture her at some high society function in Charleston. "This was our sister's home, and we are here to lay claim to what should continue in the family tradition."

Well, shit, "I'm sorry, ladies, that you came all this way. There was already a reading of Alice's will." And I had gotten everything except a few financial bequeathments, one in particular to a niece.

"We know about the reading," palm frond suit continued, "This one received a measly ten grand for college." She pointed her thumb at the young woman who had yet to speak. "What she should have received was her legacy. The will didn't tell any of us who inherited that legacy just that some nobody Soldier of Fortune was taking over the library—the library that has been in our family for centuries. I can't decide what is the worse loss—the legacy or the library."

I got the distinct impression that the legacy she referred to was none other than my unwanted mantle.

"Umm, that sounds pretty rough." I was at a loss for words as to what they expected from me.

Palm fronds glared at me, and I noticed her icy blue eyes for the first time. Just then a spirit moved behind me and whispered in my ear. "Well, she's a real bitch. No wonder Alice hated her." As the spirit moved behind me a shiver ran through my body at the sudden chill in the oppressive heat. That was all that the hawkeyed women before me needed. *My tell.*

"You," Palm frond and French braid stated in unison.

"Uh, yeah, so I am the nobody Soldier of Fortune that Alice left the library to."

"And the legacy." Palm frond went on.

Despite Deval and possibly Griselda now knowing my secret, the months of hammering into me that I needed to keep it a secret stopped me from saying anything.

"Let us in the building." French braid's voice had gone down an octave and her entire stance changed. This woman had no problem with brawling with a woman half her age in the middle of a street of hot asphalt.

"So, yeah, not sure how comfortable I am with that. I'm Peg, by the way. I am so sorry for your loss. We all loved Alice dearly..." I let my own rushed words trail off.

"Pleasure," Palm frond said though her tone suggested otherwise.

"Umm, nice to meet you. I'm Adelaide and she's Petunia," the young woman finally spoke while gesturing to palm frond, "And she's Carlita," she pointed to French braid.

It was a lifeline, and I grasped for it.

"So nice to meet all of you. You know I'd love to maybe set up a meeting, maybe a dinner where we could, ya know, hash some of this out. I'd hate to do anything to upset Alice's family. Right now though, I just remembered a work thing. Pleasure to meet all of you!"

Carlita took a step forward as if to rush me, and I took that as an opportunity to pivot on the ball of my foot and leap from the sidewalk back to my parking space to get in my car quickly as I heard footsteps pounding behind me. I managed to get in the car and turn the key in the ignition before Carlita got to me. She slammed her palm onto the hood of my Jeep as I backed out hurriedly but didn't pursue me any further. I scalded my hand trying to buckle my seatbelt and drive, but I managed to do both.

The ghost who'd spoken to me before had settled into the passenger seat of my seventies vintage Jeep Grand Cherokee.

"Lucky for you, I was nosy in life, and I'm even nosier in the after life, and do I have some hot goss for you."

It was strange to see a ghost in what appeared to be clothing from the early nineteen hundreds use such modern vernacular, but honestly, finally a ghost I wanted to talk to.

I learned on my drive home that my new buddy's name was Mallory. She stared out of the window the majority of the ride back to my house humming a jaunty tune that sounded centuries old. She didn't seem chatty, and I enjoyed the quiet company. When I finally pulled my car in my driveway, I noted that there were two goblin-issue SUVs still parked out front. I sighed and turned to Mallory.

"I may be a few minutes, but I'm actually going back to the library ruins through a back door I have that you can't enter. I don't really know how ghost travel works, but would you be able to return there to speak with me?"

"Won't be a problem at all," she responded with a nod and with that she began to shimmer and fade, sending a sweeping burst of cold throughout my car.

If my AC ever went out, I could bribe the ghosts with promises of murder to shimmy in and out of existence to keep my home cool. I shrugged to myself, got out of my car, and headed to my side gate to see what was happening.

As I had suspected, the two black SUVs did in fact belong to goblins. Goblins who had obviously drained my other pool and absconded with it. I would have complained if it weren't for the two beefy specimens currently using an air pump to set up a new one. One of the two men in suits caught sight of me and yelled over the sound of the air compressor.

"The prince wanted you to know that he got you a new play pool with a better pump this time."

I gave the man a brittle smile and walked in my back door. I didn't need any criticisms regarding my choice in "play" pools as Deval had surely emphasized. There was only one thing to do now. Sneak into the library without another forced interaction with Alice's family.

I entered George through the magical goblin safe I had sitting in my living room. I raised the lid of the elaborate metal chest was made of a million dollars worth of precious metals but beyond its materials, it was priceless. The bottom of the box had turned from a solid floor into a steep set of stone steps as soon as I placed my foot inside. I'd accidentally become the "owner" of George on my first big gig as a fortune. The chest had been stolen from Deval and used as a combination asphyxiation device-slash-coffin. I'd brought it home as evidence only to be attacked by Deval and accused of theft. Long story short, while investigating the chest, or goblin plane now known as George, my dormant goblin heritage had awakened, and the chest had bonded with me instead of Deval.

The safe itself should have been the only entrance into George, the purple rock semi-wasteland semi-chilly vibes of a plane, but my witch and goblin magic had combined in a true life or death display of power battling the leaders of the Arizona and New Mexico vampire sects. They'd both died and Pammy, my mentor and head of the Arizona witches, was currently in New Mexico dealing with the fallout there. So far, resulting fallout hadn't touched me, but I think that had more to do with Pammy protecting me than it did with any vampire kindness. Nature's purest psychopaths didn't tend to think of things in terms of what a reasonable reaction would be to having someone murdered in front of them and having one's own life threatened.

After crossing the plane's rural, windy, tundra-like atmosphere for fifteen minutes, I came to a door that stood in the middle of nothing. It was a solid brown wood door with a brass handle. There was no lock on the knob but a single deadbolt on the door itself. Around the door where a wall should have been, my own magics had twisted into a rope, green for the witch magic, flecks of goblin gold and bronze shimmer licking the outside, and now a strand of purple from the death reader mantle.

I reached out and flung the deadbolt open. I didn't think that the physical manifestation of the lock was actually necessary, only I could enter my plane without an invitation, but I also thought that my psyche had wanted me to feel safe. The reassuring heavy click of undoing the bolt kept my mind at ease. Once more there was a set of stone steps. I ascended them, happy for the lift in my rear, but disappointed in the amount of huffing and puffing I needed to do to reach the top.

I stepped into the courtyard and moved forward. The stairs disappeared, and I turned to see the door once more in my magic's mind eye. There was another deadbolt, which I then stepped toward and set in place. From a safety standpoint, it wouldn't make sense to have a deadbolt that locked in two separate places, but I knew that my magic had designed it to follow me, meaning that nothing else could follow me in or out of my plane unless I allowed it to do so.

I entered the building. I thought about going to the

front door to see if Alice's family remained, but I worried they would hear me on the other side, so, instead, I walked lightly across the floor and quietly climbed the carpeted steps up to the midlevel landing that I knew had a small circular window that would allow me to determine if they were still below. The little alcove at the front door was empty. I let out a deep breath. I didn't know what to say to a group of disgruntled women over an inheritance that I hadn't expected or even wanted but still felt oddly responsible for.

That business done, I walked up the remaining flight of stairs to the actual library of the building. Even though the plushly carpeted stairs muffled my footsteps, I continued to walk softly, paranoid that the women had found a way in, and that the peaceful oasis would turn into a hair-pulling brawl reminiscent of the old talk show moderated by Jerry Springer which was known for over-the-top fighting from all of the guests.

I looked around warily. Everything remained still. I rolled my neck releasing the tension that had gathered. Only a few months ago, I would have kept myself to three locations in the building. Even though it was known as "the library" and a place for witches to research, it was also Alice's home. I stayed in the library itself, a guest restroom nearby, or the second story kitchen that she had graciously set up as a communal space. She'd even left out snacks for people. Yet, another reason I had no business running the library. I was very selfish when it came to food, and if I ever did find the recipe for Alice's amazing cinnamon bread, I wasn't so sure I'd be willing to share the finished product.

Concerns for another day, I reminded myself as I walked along the railing on the landing to the right of the actual library and then past the bathroom and kitchen entrances to take a right at the far end into a narrower and darker space that dead ended at a small door. Like other private places in the home, this door was keyed through wards. Alice had done the wards and the keying, and I still couldn't figure out how they all worked.

Instead of worrying about the how, I just set my hand against the door and felt the magic snap forward and hold it there like a firm but not painful vise. The magic traveled through my body, inspecting me and seeking out any tricksters. After about fifteen seconds of this, the magic released me, and I heard a snick of the lock releasing. I stepped inside the crowded office and closed the door behind me. That way if anyone else still able to access the library came, I would remain undisturbed. The ruin did a good job of keeping people out of spaces where they didn't belong.

I took off the cross-body purse that I had brought and set it down on the crowded desk. The room was small, especially compared to the other more cavernous spaces in the building, maybe nine by eleven, but the ceiling was taller than the architecture of the building suggested it should be. Maybe twenty-five feet tall. Every wall was a jam-packed bookshelf all the way to the ceiling and a spindly yet deceptively strong rolling ladder facilitated access to the papers, journals, and books in the overfilled shelves. Other than that there was a fireplace, quite the fire hazard in the small space of kindling, a heavy wooden desk in front of that fireplace, and an armchair by a stained glass window. I couldn't see this window from anywhere outside the building, but when it rained, the window got wet. One day I'd figure that one out.

I sat down at the desk and looked around me. One moment the room was empty and the next moment I saw Mallory. My hand flew to my chest.

"I'd have thought you would be used to us by now," she commented, her tone dry.

"You'd think, but I would say that as a whole ghosts aren't ones for proper etiquette, and the whole being swarmed on a regular basis hasn't really allowed for regular conversations."

"That and the current group you attract are all of the truly insane."

"Huh?" I mean I knew that but she implied that there were other less homicidal spirits that hadn't stopped by to say "Hi."

"Is that a question?"

"I mean, you're the one who brought it up."

"Very well, the ones that come around right now are the ones that do not care for your personal well being. They only care that you are fresh meat, more vulnerable, and they believe perhaps they can accomplish with you what they failed to do with Alice."

"Logical enough," I agreed.

"There are, of course, others. People who are stuck here but for less disturbing reasons, and they are allowing you to gather your bearings before they approach. Unfortunately, you have taken longer than most to acclimate to your new calling."

I scowled at the faded figure before me. "It's not that easy to be constantly bombarded by the otherworld." I sounded as defensive as I felt.

"I'm sure it's discombobulating to say the least, but in the more recent decades the Belgardes have passed the mantle among themselves. This has allowed the new carriers an advantage in knowing tips and tricks to dispel us when necessary. You stumbled on a few yourself, water, that goblin contraption. There are other tricks used by pure witches, but they are unnecessary for you, with the magic your suitor showed you earlier."

I considered correcting her on my relationship status with Deval but decided it would be difficult to explain, given that I didn't have any clear definitions myself.

"Well, I'm glad I'm finally getting in the game. I'm curious why the tricks a witch death reader would use weren't in any of Alice's personal papers?"

She looked pointedly up and around the room at the thousands of documents. "You've studied all of these along with the other books throughout the home?"

I reddened a little. "I've done a fair amount when I wasn't being forced into a trance."

"Perhaps it doesn't matter that you have not been able to look into all of these sources. She may have simply kept the tricks to an oral tradition, though I would find that odd given that she did not speak to you of this despite knowing that she planned on breaking with tradition and passing the mantle to you. She straight up cut off the fam." Mallory once again surprised me by switching to modern slang.

"Well, I don't know what's going on with the 'fam,' but I do know that Deval has asked me for a favor, and I would like to help him if I'm able. I would need a few spirits, though, frankly, one is better than none, to find and spy on these goblin mercenaries that have come to town."

"That could be arranged certainly, and you're willing to exchange favors in return?"

"I will need to hear specific favors before I agree to the exchange. I don't need any bait-and-switch scenarios, and it only takes a little bit of common sense to realize that I have absolutely no interest in committing any felonies. I might be willing to do a misdemeanor if my chances of being caught are low enough."

"Understood. I shall bring by candidates tomorrow."

"And what is your price——?"

And just like that Mallory popped out of existence, sans the shimmy this time, before I could ask her price. *That probably wasn't great.*

4

The next morning, I woke up late to the sound of Cheddar growling from my side. I lifted the pillow that I'd draped over my head, to cut out extraneous noise and light but also to give any would-be murderers a helping hand at smothering me, and looked at my cat. Usually he woke me up just to let me know I'd missed breakfast time, so I was surprised to see my bed circled by six spirits. No wonder the air conditioner felt extra powerful this morning. Cheddar did not like it and neither did I: the ghosts, not the air conditioning.

"For the most part, y'all have left me alone while I sleep. I really enjoyed that as an unspoken rule, and I would prefer to keep it. Plus, not to be a bitch or anything, I'm sure being dead and left to roam the earth is no picnic, but I found out about this buzzing thing yesterday and I'm not afraid to buzz y'all."

"Madam said you requested our presence." A gentlemanly figure stepped forward. His voice said upper crust but his forties-era clothing said field hand. There was a story there.

"Madam?" I asked.

"A Ms. Mallory said you'd trade reasonable favors for spy work."

"Ah." I rotated and pushed myself up on my forearms before scooting back against the headboard. Cheddar hissed again, this time at me, but he resettled on my lap rather than run the gauntlet through the wall of ghosts.

"We have a list of requests in return for service."

"Hit me with it," I said and reached out to scratch behind Cheddar's ears. A deep rumbling purr started, but he simultaneously twitched his tail in irritation at the intruders.

"Of the six of us, there are two who would request that you take down a correspondence and deliver it to a loved one. One that wishes you to communicate her murderer to the proper authorities. Another would like you to drive up north and dig up an antique tea set she had buried. She did not wish for her cousin to get her filthy paws on Meemaw's good china, but she also does not wish for it to decompose. One is doing it simply to pass the time and will request no favors in return. Finally, my wish is for you to bake my recipe of orange rolls and deliver them to my daughter who lives in a nursing home near Tucson. Dementia is a nasty disease, and I want to make her happy."

I had a little tug to the heartstrings on the last request, but I was leery because they were all such reasonable requests and that had not been my experience thus far.

"Is there a time frame we're looking to accomplish all this? How far north are we talking for the china?"

"We do not need payment in advance, but we do request that these requests be completed within the next thirty days. The dishes are outside of Flagstaff."

The small university town was only a three-hour drive

and nearly six thousand feet in elevation difference away. It would actually be a nice day or weekend trip.

"And the person with no request. How can I be certain this person is not going to come looking to have me murder a litter of puppies six years from now?"

"You have a rather bad opinion of us as a whole, but I can guarantee that Patrice regularly performed favors for Alice in the past, just for the fun of it."

A faded figure of a woman, short, plump, with rounded ruddy cheeks, well, more of a light pink given her state of being stepped forward and nodded. She was wearing more modern clothes than the rest of the bunch, with high-waisted western jeans painted on her figure and a western-style button-up. If her clothes didn't say it, the once red, now a faded strawberry blonde, hair Aquanetted within an inch of its life screamed late eighties early nineties.

"You sure, Patrice? No takes backsies?"

"No takes backsies," she agreed.

Before I could further grill them on the intricacies of what I was agreeing to, I felt a disturbance in my wards. The house itself was locked to those not invited in, but I had added additional warning chimes halfway down the front path and on the porch. It had initially been to warn me when any nut-job vampires showed up with flowers, that problem was solved for now at least by my killing Fane Dimir, but I still knew when strangers approached. The doorbell rang.

I reached out and unceremoniously deposited Cheddar beside me and swung my legs around to stand up. I held out a finger to my company and walked through Patrice who stood between me and my bedroom door, shivering as I did so.

"Excuse me just a minute. Don't y'all go anywhere!" I

called behind me as I looked down to inspect my current situation. Tank top and pajama shorts. I wasn't wearing a bra, but the material was thick enough that I didn't feel weird about it. I reached up and felt my curls. Still haphazardly in the bun from the night before but definitely some not-so-tamed pieces sticking up at intervals. Eh, what could you do?

At the door, I looked through peephole and nearly took a step back. I hadn't expected the man who I suspected of putting a dead body in my pool to just show up on my front stoop the next day.

"Hello, Gregar," I spoke in a high friendly voice while I simultaneously swung the door open and primed my magic. I looked to my palm and saw the green and purple twisted up my wrist eager to knock a bitch back. I looked up and met his eyes. He did not look happy to see me despite the smile on his face.

"Ms. Darrow," his tone was oddly high pitched as well, probably the strain of being polite to me.

I already despised him, but Deval called me that and I didn't like it coming from his cousin. I could feel the corners of my mouth pinching.

"Hi, come to throw a body in my pool? Maybe turn yourself in for the murder of your own brother? I'm pretty sure Deval would really like to have a reunion."

Something flashed in his eyes. Could have been anger. Could have been goblin magic, even though he hadn't gone full molten metal. It was probably both, but he let his eyes go flat. Never a great sign.

"I would think that since you are no longer involved with my cousin that you might be interested in what I have to offer."

I glanced behind him at his two bodyguards. They

looked like something out some Special Forces unit, the Hollywood version. Cargo pants, tight T-shirts, boots, sunglasses, closely cropped hair, and all of it black, which brought out the mildly gray undertone in their skin.

"What exactly is it that you're offering and don't they know better to wear all black in an Arizona summer?"

Gregar's jaw clenched, but the men behind him remained completely void of any facial expression.

"They are dressed just fine for their duties. And I am offering you far more than you deserve. You are not wholly goblin. How you managed to secure a plane in our realms is beyond me, but my father and I have agreed to let you keep it after we depose my aunt."

I literally felt the click of the door between my and George's connection open ever so slightly. Someone was being nosy, and I couldn't blame him.

"Okay, and what exactly would you expect in return for treason?"

"You are not one of us, so you cannot be tried for treason, and in any case, Delmy would need to be the rightful heir in order for it to be treason. Ours is a patriarchal lineage, as was the strongest of the European kings."

I managed to not roll my eyes, but it was a close call. Someone had selected only the bits of history that supported their desires.

"There must, of course, always be a show of fealty to the rightful monarch to secure your place among the chosen."

"Again, what is this expectation?"

"I know that you and Deval have ended your entanglement, but we would like you to resurrect it."

"And what makes you think I have the power to do so?" I was genuinely curious.

"This morning when we dropped the enemy on your property, and you contacted the goblins, it was not a minion that arrived, but the crown prince himself. There are few who hold that much sway."

"Okay, and if I were to choose to be your little spy, how can I be sure that you actually have the manpower to do what you say? I don't want to choose the losing side."

He nodded approvingly. "And that is why you must side with the rightful heir, as a woman you must know that you are the heart of the family not the head. You have your place in the kingdom, just not at the head of the table."

"Who is this asshole?" A voice came from behind me. I didn't react, but whichever ghost said it was preaching to the choir.

"Of course, I wouldn't want to worry over your strategies, that's not my place," I echoed his words back to him. "Still, how do I know that you will be victorious?"

His eyes narrowed but he gestured behind himself at the two men. "We have secured the Beast's Folly army."

I didn't know what the Beast's Folly army was, but I widened my eyes as though I thought it was as impressive as he did. Gregar began to expound on the many victories of his mercenary army, and I looked to his hired hands to see if the praise would make them crack. It did not, but while looking at them, I noticed a Chrysler minivan pull up directly in front of my home. It looked to be from a decade or two past and the oxidized paint, which I suspected had once been a champagne color, had seen better days.

The peeling tinted windows didn't allow me to see the occupants until the three relatives of Alice climbed out. The youngest struggled to get the lock to latch and slammed the sliding back door closed several times before it properly closed. All the while Gregar droned on and only looked back at where I was staring once the women started up the path. He stiffened at the sight of the three women and turned his whole body to face them leaving me at his back. The guards changed position immediately to cover his front and back. Good to know he was getting his money's worth.

The women wore exceedingly similar outfits to the ones they had on the day before. The only significant difference was that palm frond had changed into a summer suit that sported hibiscus flowers instead and looked fresher than the melted version of herself from the previous evening. The two sisters walked side-by-side up the path, glaring daggers at the small group of goblins, while the younger one trailed behind, eyes on the ground.

"What are these people doing here?" Petunia aka hibiscus formerly known as palm fronds asked. I couldn't miss the derogatory emphasis on people. She obviously recognized the men as goblins, and she wasn't a fan. I wasn't a fan of them either, but that's because I knew they were assholes. Her instant derision obviously came from a hateful mind.

Gregar took a step forward and immediately one his guards placed a hand on his shoulder. Gregar's head snapped back to look at the man who dared restrain him. Whatever he saw there made him flush. I needed to say something before I had a brawl on my front porch.

"So nice to see you, ladies. When I said we should do dinner, I didn't mean this time of the morning." I'd never actually looked at a clock after waking. I had no idea what time of the morning it was.

"Well, you didn't stay to leave a number. We had to make our own arrangements to see you." Petunia continued up the path, skirted the goblins, giving them wide berth and stood before me. Carlita and the young woman lined up right behind her while the goblin faction shifted the guards, once again attempting to protect their boss from all angles. I didn't envy them.

I now had two groups of people I didn't want to talk to in front of me and a passel of ghosts waiting on my orders behind me. I needed to get rid of some of my uninvited guests.

"Gregar, I will think about your suggestion. Do you have a way for me to reach you?" All the while I was talking, I had put my hand behind my back and begun pointing forcefully in their general direction, hoping one of the ghosts would get the hint and follow them.

"Does this mean you agree to our favors?" A frail voice asked.

I nodded affirmatively in the smallest gesture I could make, but I saw Petunia's eyes narrow.

Gregar stared at me for a moment before reaching into his back pocket and pulling out a wallet. From it he produced a card and handed it to me.

"Do not take too long to come to the right decision." With that he turned and headed down the drive. Goosebumps covered my skin as two of my spies floated through me as I blocked the door.

Petunia's eyes widened, and I looked down to her bare arm to see that her skin had also reacted to the sudden cold.

"I don't know who you are, mister, but I'd be careful about this one. You never know when you're being watched."

Gregar paused on the walkway for a moment to look back and scowl, unfortunately his guards looked thoughtfully back at me before turning to follow the stomping would-be prince to the black SUV I now associated with goblins.

"Dick move, Petunia." My eyes had returned to the woman in front of me.

She shrugged.

"How did you get my address?"

"You should really be more careful about sweeping your vehicle. Sloppy." Carlita aka French braid and tanned legs a twenty-year-old would be jealous of stepped forward to stand next to her sister.

Gods damn it. I had a flashback to Carlita slamming her hand down on the hood of my Jeep.

"Sorry, I thought I was fleeing an awkward social situation not a couple of stalkers."

"Don't invite a Southern woman to a meal and expect her not to show up," Carlita countered.

I threw my hands up in the air. I knew when I was beaten, and I needed to get whatever this was over with, so I could move on to more important things like reclaiming my life and spying on enemy goblin armies.

"Well, I believe you said your names were Carlita and Petunia," I looked at both women in turn, "I'm sorry but can you remind me yours?" I looked to the meek person who didn't cower but just sort of disappeared behind her aunts.

"Adelaide," came a soft but strong voice.

"Adelaide," I acknowledged and nodded toward her, "Can I interest you ladies in a cup of coffee."

"Yes, we have much to discuss." Petunia moved to surge forward, but I held up my hand before my wards could zap her as an intruder. I mumbled a spell to let the women pass and gestured the women forward. The two sisters walked in as though they owned the place. Adelaide followed at a slower pace.

Leaving a front door open in triple digit weather with the air conditioning running was sacrilegious to an Arizona native, but I didn't make the "hurry up gesture" despite my strong desire to do so. When she finally made it in, I closed the door and walked to where the women stood, obviously annoyed that they had to wait for me and Adelaide. The remaining ghosts that had not followed the goblins hovered around, but they had all picked up on the fact that Petunia knew the signs of their presence and made an effort to avoid the women.

"If y'all would like to take a seat, I can go ahead and make some coffee." I gestured to my semi-cluttered living room off the entryway. Adelaide lingered but Carlita marched in and made herself comfortable on my loveseat while Petunia looked, eagle-eyed, around the room, landing on the goblin chest. She entered the room, deliberately making over exaggerated movements to avoid a couple of boxes I had left on the floor before sitting as close to the safe as possible. I didn't like it, but I didn't know what to say to make her move without coming across as unnecessarily rude, so I let it go.

"Powder room?" Adelaide asked quietly.

I pointed to the appropriate door in the hallway and proceeded to the kitchen. I took a moment to look at the card Gregar had provided. It was a heavy linen card stock, cream, expensive and had a number with the 602 Phoenix area code on it. Nothing else. I reached out with my magic to see if it had been spelled at all. I didn't want to take any risks after the embarrassment of letting my vehicle get spelled right in front of me. The card didn't respond to my magic, and I placed it in a kitchen drawer for safety. You never knew when you were going to need to contact your friendly neighborhood traitor to their family line.

After that, I focused on the task at hand. I started a pot of coffee, looked in the black-hole cupboard where I put things I never used and after knocking over a few decorative bowls, some mismatched Tupperware, and a rarely used teapot, I managed to find a serving tray my mom had pawned off on me during a visit.

On the tray, I stuck my sugar bowl, a couple of packets of Splenda, and a carton of half and half. I used to have a little cream pot to match the sugar bowl, but Cheddar had knocked it off the counter to express his general disdain about something. Additionally, I added some spoons, which matched, go me, and four coffee mugs, which did not match but were the fun, quirky types that one shouldn't expect to have a set of. The coffee finished brewing, and I filled the cups, leaving enough room for my unwanted guests to doctor their coffee, and proceeded to the living room narrowly missing Cheddar as he pranced in front of me, swatting at my legs. I still hadn't fed him yet.

Adelaide had come inside the room and sat down on the loveseat, leaving a place for me next to Petunia on my couch. I set the tray on the coffee table and made a sweeping gesture toward it.

"Uh, help yourselves."

Petunia picked up one of my favorite mugs that featured the Morton's salt girl. It wasn't until she wrinkled her nose at it that I remembered it said: "Don't be a Salty Bitch" under the image.

"Uh, yeah, gag gift from a friend." I said.

She let out an oddly delicate grunt but went about adding cream and sugar to her coffee. The other two women seemed to take that as their cue and followed suit, picking a cat mug and a Sue the T-Rex mug respectively. I grabbed the last one that said something about how the contents of the cup might be tequila and went about making my own cup. With the task complete there was, however, no way of avoiding the elephant in the room any longer, although I'd prefer to have been wearing a bra, actual clothes, and have brushed my teeth before having whatever conversation we were about to have.

"All right, I probably should have stayed and talked to y'all yesterday, but frankly you took me by surprise."

"No manners at all." Carlita mumbled.

"Uh, excuse me, you three showed up at the Library and demand I let you in. Alice never mentioned any of you, and you expect me to give up my passcode. For all I know you're just a bunch of nut jobs insisting that you're related to her."

Carlita glared at me and set her mug down on a side table so she could proceed to point her finger at me.

"Listen here, you may not have known about it, but you should have. You stole our family's legacy and our collection."

"I was under the impression that Alice had created and maintained the collection."

Carlita honest to gods turned a shade bordering on purple and opened her mouth to speak before Petunia held up a hand to quiet her.

"Alice, of course, added to the collection and maintained it. That is what the eldest of a generation does in the Belgarde family. It is then passed on to the next generation. Now Alice, Carlita, and myself did not have children, but our brother did. Adelaide here is the next of the generations and deserves her legacy. She is to be the next death reader and maintainer of the documents."

I gripped my mug with both hands but remained quiet. Before there'd been the allusion to the mantle, but they hadn't outright said it. I'd gone through four months of torture not telling anyone and coming in and out of the catatonic state that I was constantly getting stuck in when barraged by the spirits. Now, in less than forty-eight hours it felt like everyone knew and even though I was relieved, I also knew that was dangerous.

"I was under the impression that this was not something to be talked about since it is dangerous to the holder of the mantle."

"Oh, posh." Petunia set down her own mug and made a dismissive gesture with her hand. "We are not discussing this openly. We are discussing it within our family, which is very much aware of the danger associated with the mantle. And we're discussing it with a naive young woman who had the unfortunate fate to be near Alice during her untimely passing. We do not blame you, since we know it was not in your control. We do, however, ask that you pass it along accordingly, and that you respect the fact that Alice had no right to leave you the book and document collection. I'm assuming she wished, for convenience, to keep it in this state rather than have us deal with the burden of moving the items back to Alabama. We will manage. You of course can keep that ruin that she has spelled to high heaven."

"Yeah, I hear what you're saying, and I do truly empathize with the disappointment, but it wasn't an accident that Alice left the mantle to me. She deliberately invited me over to ensure that I was the recipient of it. Now, as I'm sure you ladies are aware, this calling is no walk in the park. I'm not sure exactly why Alice chose me, though there was some mention of ghost soothsayers and the like. In any case, even though I'm not sure how I feel about the death reader lifestyle, the alternative is to die young and pass on the mantle."

"There is a way to pass it on. Dangerous though it may be, it is unlikely to kill you permanently, and you can do right by Adelaide." Petunia had shifted toward me her knees pressed together and gestured in my direction with her hands clasped in supplication.

"Not going to happen." I didn't have to think hard to know what they were talking about. "I've already had to take Reaper out of necessity and survived. I know that with each dosing one's odds of not waking up increases."

"But you were willing to take it before?" Adelaide asked barely above a whisper from the loveseat.

"Yes, I took it because I was going to die from a death curse otherwise. I am not going to take it to appease y'all."

I glared at the young woman and she quickly lowered her eyes.

"It is not appeasement. It is what's owed to my family. We have held the mantle for centuries."

I shook my head remembering my conversation with Deval. "Do you have goblins in the family? I know that the mantle has not always been held by the Belgardes."

"Thieves," Carlita spat out with vehemence.

Great. I've opened another can of worms. I could kick myself for even bringing it up, but between my own research and my conversation, I knew there had been times when people outside Alice's family were death readers.

"Ladies, let's go ahead and save ourselves some time. I will not be taking reaper or be willingly killed even if temporarily. I may not enjoy the responsibility, but Alice wanted me to have it for a reason. I don't know that reason yet, but I'm going to respect her final wishes."

Petunia stood and went about dusting off invisible lint from her suit while she spoke. Her family stood with her.

"I thought you might be difficult and since Arizona is currently without a sheriff, I had no choice but to get my ducks in a row." She grabbed her flamingo pink purse and dug around inside. She found what she had been looking for and shoved a heavy if somewhat wrinkled envelope at me. "Can't expect goblin-witch filth to do what's right." She finished as I was looking over the envelope.

"You've been served!" Her voice had gone shrill as she marched past me. Her sister and niece followed. Out the front door they went, slamming the door behind them.

What the actual fuck.

5

I called Pammy's number while staring at the documents.

"What is it, Sug?" Pammy answered with her usual shortened "sugar" endearment.

"I've been served."

She didn't miss a beat. "What kind of served? Court served, martini served, sport served? I am in the middle of making sure we don't have rogue vampires coming to kill us in our beds. I don't have time for this, Peg."

"I'm sorry, arbitrator served." Worry twisted in my stomach at the thought of Pammy cleaning up my mess. I knew it was technically her job, but if I hadn't killed Fane and Crina she wouldn't be in New Mexico dealing with the fallout.

"Who waited for me to leave the state to arbitrate your ass?"

"Alice's family. They want me to take Reaper to pass the death reader mantle to their family and give them all of Alice's books."

"How do they know you have the mantle?"

"They ambushed me at the library and put a tracker on my car when they came here they picked up on some signs, plus with Alice leaving the library to me, I think they already suspected."

"So now three more people know about your new party trick?"

"Four," I mumbled into the phone.

"Speak clearly."

"Four people know, Deval found me in a trance and recognized the symptoms when I found a dead goblin in my pool."

"I'm sorry did you say you found a dead goblin in your play pool?"

"Uh yeah, I was going to call you about that but a lot has happened over the last twenty-four hours."

"Tell me everything and leave nothing out."

I ran Pammy through the last day and didn't skip a single detail from the being found in a bikini, to the new found buzzing spell, my new band of ghost spies, and the goblin war.

"Well, shit on toast," Pammy said after a moment of silence.

"Yeah, that covers it."

"How do you feel knowing that you will now be living openly with powers that people will want to kill you for?"

"I mean Deval knows, and Alice's family, but they kept her secret…"

"They kept her secret because she was family, but they want you to literally kill yourself for them. They won't keep this secret, and even if they did, they've involved the arbitrator and those cases are too high profile to be kept secret."

"High profile?" I asked a little confused.

"You are probably too young. When a state has a less-than-stable sheriff, the arbitrator is used more often. Arbitrators are summoned and travel around the country, settling disputes following global witch laws, which will not take into account the idiosyncrasies that occur in individual countries and states. Long story short, whenever Yvette Sarcona comes to town, it's all over the gossip witch blogs."

"That can't be true. If my mom had read about my being served, she would have already called me."

"You were just served, dummy. It will make the blogs. Everyone and his Uncle Fred will know you carry the death reader mantle. Your life would have been easier if we'd been able to keep the cat in the bag, but it's out and announcing itself like a tom who smells a female in heat."

My stomach rolled, and I placed my hand on it to settle it. I didn't want to live a life where I was constantly worried whether someone was trying to murder me, well at least not more so than I would if I was just a regular Soldier of Fortune.

"You've gone quiet on me, Peg. Coulda, woulda, shoulda is all fine and dandy, but it's not going to help you, and I don't know if there is way that you could have gotten around this to begin with. The Belgardes want their legacy, and Alice had her reasons for not passing it on to them. Right now, we need to worry about what we can fix. Did you take that tracker off your car yet?"

"No, I'm still in my pajamas," I said quietly into the phone.

Pammy stayed silent for a beat. "You hosted a goblin traitor and a passel of murder-hungry witches in your night dress?"

"They woke me up." I considered letting her know it was a short and tank top set but decided to let the small details slide.

"Fine. So, now you're going to get dressed. You're

going to remove that tracker. You will double-check your wards. I don't like that you've had that many enemies at your home. Once you have time, I'd strongly suggest you expand your wards into your yard. Ain't no reason the goblins should have been able to just dump a corpse in your kiddie pool."

I didn't correct her.

"When is your arbitration?"

"Tomorrow morning."

"Well, then I suggest you let any close friends or family know about your new woo-woo shit because they will be hearing about it soon enough."

"Great." I managed, not sure how to throw a "Surprise! I talk to ghosts now!" for my nearest and dearest in under twelve hours.

"I know it's a pain in the ass, but do you want them to find out another way?"

"No."

"Good, now keep me informed. I don't like the goblins pulling you into their war, but it would be a nice chip to cash in if we ever need their help."

"We?"

"You may be part goblin, but you're a witch first and don't think for a minute I wouldn't be willing to call in your chip if it came down to it."

My stomach lurched again. "Are things going that poorly in New Mexico?"

"They are going as good as can be expected. Mind you, even if you hadn't killed two reigning vampires in the Southwest, vampires could have attacked us at anytime. It was just less likely. If they don't choose a new ruler here soon, I may need to go to Texas and tell them the New Mexico sect is gunning for them, rile them up so they can fight among themselves for a bit. It's always best for us when they're fighting among themselves and not worried about witches."

"That sounds complicated."

"Authoritarian regimes are complicated."

"I'll take your word for it."

"Now get off this phone and try to figure some of your shit out."

"Yes, ma'am."

When I got off the phone, I'd immediately called Lola. She was on her way back from a job site on the outskirts of Tucson but agreed to come right over once she made it back home. Lola had bought a home near mine a few months ago, which had come in very handy when I hadn't answered my phone a few times when stuck in a trance. The new unspoken rule had been if I didn't return a missed call within an hour, she would just show up. A few times she'd gotten me out of a trance and a couple of times she'd either woken me up in the middle of a nap or scared the bejeezus out of me when I'd been taking a shower.

While I waited for her, I started the very reasonable list that Pammy had provided. Get out of pajamas? Check. Remove tracker spell from Jeep? Got zapped by a kickback in the process and my fingers still stung, but check! Tell my parents about the death reader mantle? Soon. Ward the backyard? Not so much.

Despite the upkeep, I loved my yard. I was one of the lucky few who had irrigation for my lot, which meant abundant citrus trees and grass, though right now every-thing was looking pretty crispy. I traded the tank top and short pajamas for a tank top that did not have "Sleepy

Time" emblazoned across my chest and a pair of denim cutoffs. The baseball cap and sunglasses helped a little against the blazing sun but not much as I analyzed the work it would take to fully ward my yard. I had done my own warding on the house, and that had been tedious enough when the temperatures weren't triple digits.

I wanted to do anything but the task before me, so when the air turned icy, raising bumps on my exposed skin, I was happy to find my unofficial ghost posse floating toward me. The jaunty fellow who'd brokered the deal and Patrice came forward leaving the other four to look at me with what I thought was trepidation from a distance, but shadowy figures were hard to read.

"We have been foiled, Miss." The man stood before me wringing his hands.

Patrice looked at the ground moving the toe of her pointed cowboy boot as though to flatten grass. It of course did not flatten.

"Foiled?" I asked.

"They used countermeasures. I attempted to ride along with some of them, and they were none the wiser at first. This dreadful climate!" The last statement came out as an exclamation before the ghost covered his face dramatically.

Patrice looked up from her toe. "What Fred is trying to say is that it's easier to suss us out in this weather. They didn't know we joined their car ride because the driver had stayed in the car and kept the air-conditioning running at your place, but they stopped for lunch and the driver went inside with them. Once they got in the car once more, they knew immediately.

"One of them had a bottle of salt spray with him, and they soused us! Oh, how it burned!" Fred rejoined the conversation.

"I didn't know that worked. You mean I could have just

mixed some salt water together in a spray bottle all these months?"

"It is uncomfortable but nothing like the buzzy thing you did." Patrice gave Fred a pained look at his dramatics. "Did you know they even sell it now for hair styling? We were hosed down with Salty Beach Wave spray. We would have persevered, but they began to do the vibration thing when the car remained cold." Patrice provided the additional information.

"That is a little strange." I said thinking specifically of the two mercenaries with closely cropped hair.

"I thought so, too, but the driver had what must be a luscious mane pulled back in a tight braid. When he's off duty, I could definitely picture him having some Fabio moments." Patrice understood my confusion. Her Fabio comment also cemented my suspicion of her being a lady from the eighties.

"I didn't see him." I was oddly intrigued by the would-be romance cover model who worked as a mercenary to pay the bills.

"I did," Patrice said. Frankly she seemed about to swoon, if ghosts could even do that.

"Get yourself together, woman." Fred had apparently recovered from his own theatrics, so that he could rain on his counterpart's parade.

The two ghosts glared at each other.

"Hey, now, no need to worry. We didn't think it would be this easy did we?" I asked.

"It usually isn't," Fred mumbled.

"It never is." I pushed the point home. "I'm new to this whole communing with the spirits thing, but even I know that nothing is ever as easy as we think it's gonna be."

"Of course not, Miss." Fred stood a little straighter while Patrice rolled her eyes. I wasn't sure if it was at me or at Fred, so I decided it was best to ignore it. Pep talks weren't for everyone.

"Okay, so how do you guys usually go about finding people to spy on?"

"Under normal circumstances, we would stake out known associates. The problem is his known associates are in hiding with him. All of his friends and acquaintances would become suspicious to Delmy. She's an astute woman and not afraid of delivering a strong punishment," Patrice said.

"How do you know so much about the comings and goings of the goblin court?" I asked.

"They are very interesting to watch," Fred supplied. "They, of course, don't have the same level of drama and machinations as the vampires, but there is considerably less gore and torture, which can be upsetting to one's mental state."

I nodded. I could only imagine.

"We can, of course, place our people at the court and hope for contact as well as in places Gregar was known to visit in the past," Fred continued.

I shook my head in the negative.

"I have a better idea. You said the only reason they figured out how to repel you was because they felt you in the car, right?"

"Yes," the ghosts said in unison.

"So, if I set up a meeting with Gregar, skip the meeting, and instead follow him, you could hitch a ride with me, and I can drop you off there. Then you can keep an appropriate distance and spy on him?"

"That is a sound plan, Miss."

"Great, I just need to cancel on Lola."

And that was how, two hours later, I sat in the parking lot of Bump and Grind Cafe with a Jeep full of ghosts. We'd parked toward the back. A catering van for a BBQ joint, painted to resemble a pig blocked us from view, but I still had good visibility of the coffee shop. The bright side of taxiing around a group of the deceased was that I didn't need to turn on the AC which helped, given my Jeep's a gas-guzzler status. In fact, the vehicle had become cold to the point that I had rolled the windows down, hoping for a hot breeze. When I'd arrived thirty minutes early to purchase a latte, I'd gone ahead and gotten the drink hot, knowing what my stakeout consisted of. Only in Arizona would a barista give you an odd look for ordering your coffee hot.

Gregar had been eager to meet when I told him I thought I could help him but had just woken up earlier and wasn't thinking clearly, and he had even agreed to meet me at the unofficial witch headquarters, the Bump and Grind Café. I'd been surprised by that and had only thrown it out as a place to start location negotiations. My final goal had been any random coffee shop in the greater Phoenix area that allowed me to get there early enough to get a coffee and make an appearance indoors, so if Gregar asked around he would hear that I had been there and would assume I'd gotten cold feet.

Now, whereas I had been thirty minutes early to set my little plan in motion, I looked at my phone and saw that Gregar was ten minutes late. It didn't surprise me. He wasn't the type to keep prompt appointments on his end. He thought too highly of himself, though he would be the first person to bitch if you showed him the same level of discourtesy. I'd started to play I Spy with the ghosts and was thankful when Gregar finally made an appearance because I could not for the life of me spot something purple; the ghosts latest hint in our game. He and the same two bodyguards were let out of a nondescript SUV right in front of the cafe.

"All right, game is over. They're here!" I told the ghosts.

I had considered placing a tracker spell on the SUV a la the same spell Carlita had slapped on my hood, but that plan was foiled by what appeared to be a very alert driver. My phone began to buzz and sure enough the number from the card appeared on my caller ID. I sent it to voice-mail and continued to do so for the next eight calls that came through. I also received several text messages that started polite and turned colorful quickly.

He didn't last fifteen minutes before he left the coffee shop looking pissed. I waited until he got into the car before I turned over my engine. My vehicle had the sort of engine that made a loud purr when I turned it on and the goal was to not attract attention, difficult enough in a brightly painted vintage Jeep.

I pulled out slowly and began to follow the SUV at a respectable distance. I hadn't really thought through the logistics of following someone in my particularly noticeable vehicle until we'd already committed to this plan. I'd considered getting a more non-descript car in the past, just a cheap older sedan for such purposes, but as I hadn't really been on my "A" game these past few months, this idea had fallen by the wayside.

Ten minutes later we were on the 60 headed east, and our prey seemed none the wiser for our tail. I stayed a good distance back. The nice thing about this particular freeway in the middle of the afternoon was that it was a wide, open space where I could see far off into the distance, and all of the exit ramps were very visible. The ghosts chattered all around me and seemed particularly thrilled about our little mission. The ghosts gave me all their names, but I'd already forgotten the lot of them other than Patrice and Fred.

I needed individual interactions to cement the names, but it did make me feel a little awkward about car interactions, so instead of taking the time to learn everyone's names I asked if they minded if I turned on a podcast. They didn't and like a good portion of the population, they became entranced as the podcast hosts told the story of a particularly brutal murder and the subsequent manhunt.

Despite being enthralled by the podcast myself, I knew that I needed to keep my eyes on the prize as the further east we went, the sparser the traffic around me became. The goblin vehicle didn't make any evasive moves, so I assumed we were still in the all clear. About thirty minutes in, they took exit 212 and I let out a groan.

"Noooooooo."

"What is it, Miss?" Fred reached forward as to pause the chatter on speakers, but his hand went through the vehicle. I reached over and did it for him. I still didn't understand ghost physics. They were all perched on seats in the vehicle, but they couldn't touch a button?

"I know this route, and we're just taking a longer road trip than I'd planned."

"Where are we going?"

"Either Florence or Tucson."

One was known for a prison and affordable housing off the beaten path; the other was home of one of the three major state universities and also where my parents lived. If we did end up in Tucson, I was going definitely going to visit my parents to give then the whole story: "Your daughter talks to ghosts and will likely be hunted her entire life for that power!" That and raid their deep freeze and steal a bag of tamales. It didn't matter how old I got, the privilege of a child visiting their parents was to steal their food.

"That would be quite the distance, Miss," Fred said.

"I'm guessing Florence. He's been in and around Phoenix too much to be making the drive to Tucson every day," I said, hopeful. I'd like to see my parents, but I had arbitration in the morning.

"It's only a two-hour drive to Tucson, and the city has amenities that he partakes of on a regular basis," one of the nameless ghosts with a thick drawl offered from behind me.

"We'll end up where we end up," I said, keeping my eyes forward and my hands at ten and two. We were on a pretty deserted section of the road, and I didn't want to stay too close or be spotted. "But we all need to admit that no one would expect to find Gregar in Florence. He likes cigars, strip clubs, and anything considered high-end. "There are a lot of nice things about Florence, but I don't think it offers those things."

"More quaint surroundings to be sure," Fred agreed with me.

The SUV in front of me took an exit for Butte Road, and I let out a sigh of relief. I hadn't planned on making the trip to Tucson today, and the last thing I wanted to do was to run out of gas on a rural highway. The more rural areas tended to be less friendly toward witches, in my experience. Not that anyone would know I was a witch on sight, but the thought of being out of gas and "helpless" in the middle of nowhere did not appeal to me.

As we exited, I noted the sign that advised people not to pick up hitchhikers. Good advice given the number of correctional facilities in the eight-mile city.

"Keep an eye on the SUV, guys. I need to fall back even more."

The ghosts stayed silent, but when I glanced over, their hazy forms held perfectly still, eyes forward.

"Best to look forward, Miss," Fred commented, his tone dry.

I did and my heart jumped out of my chest as I slammed on my breaks. My old metal bucket stopped, but I had to be one inch away from rear-ending a Dodge Neon that had once been purple but now was a sun-bleached lavender. A vehicle behind me laid on its own horn and wouldn't let up. I glared into my rearview mirror at the giant diesel truck behind me and I considered flipping the bird but decided against it. The area was a little too gun happy for me to freely insult people via hand gestures.

"The car's moved, and we're losing them." Patrice brought my focus back to the task at hand.

"Shit," I muttered and pulled forward to the stop sign that I'd missed earlier. There were no other cars at the intersection, so I pulled a California stop, barely braking before speeding forward.

"Do you know where they went?" I asked trying to keep the mild panic from my voice as my eyes darted around the road.

"Make the second right up ahead at that building that looks like a saloon," one of the backseat ghosts called out.

I made the turn and slammed down on my brakes once more. A burning scent filled the Jeep from my abused brakes. A goblin stood in the middle of the road. I recognized him as one of Gregar's bodyguards from the elite militia, but that wasn't what scared me. His eyes glowed like molten metal, and I could sense the slightest tremor from the ground. He was pulling his magic right here in broad daylight. My eyes darted around. I didn't see any civilians, but I saw windows, and there had to be security cameras on some of the businesses. I didn't know what to do, and I froze.

"Miss, you must flee. We will follow the scoundrel from here on foot!" Fred spoke in a stage whisper and from one breath to the next, my car interior went from frozen to stiflingly hot. I made eye contact with the goblin in front of me and threw my car in reverse. I screeched backward, sending a little prayer to all the gods as I backed blindly into an intersection. When there was no impact, I took my eyes off the goblin and put my car in drive, hitting the gas pedal. My tires let out another shriek, and now a smell of burnt rubber filled the compartment to compliment the odor of burnt brakes. I didn't care.

My mission had been accomplished, and as far as I knew I'd managed to not unwittingly be party to exposing the goblin population to the humans. I needed to call Deval and tell him that his cousin's militia didn't have too many qualms about outing themselves. But first I needed to figure out how to tell my mom that I'd been able to talk to ghosts for the last four months, and why I hadn't told her. Definitely not looking forward to that conversation.

My brilliant plan of simply texting my close friends and family my news, aka the coward's way out, was thwarted by my very well intentioned best friend. When I pulled up to my house, I saw Bruce's beast of a truck parked out front. Where Bruce went these days, Lola followed, and vice versa, at least that had been my observation when I wasn't in a near-constant ghost-coma state, and tonight seemed no different. When I walked up to my home, I didn't have a chance to even feel my wards before Lola threw my front door open.

"It's your coming out party!" She exclaimed holding her hands out and wiggling her fingers.

Bruce came up behind her in my doorway and mouthed "sorry" but I didn't think it was too sincere given the twinkle in his eyes.

"Lola," I asked cautiously, "What have you done?"

"Okay, so it's not really a party just me, and Bruce, and your parents on Zoom. Your sister couldn't make it to the Zoom call, but your mom has assured me she will let her know what the big news is once she's heard about it."

"You really didn't have to do this, Lola," I said trying to keep the irritation out of my voice and simultaneously relax my jaw, which had begun to tense.

"I know and I know that you're probably mad, but now you can get it over in one quick ripping off the Band-Aid!" She made a hand gesture ushering me into my own house, and I followed her because she was right, and it was time to rip off the Band-Aid.

Bruce had lingered behind to walk with me the whole two feet into the living room.

"Has she told you?" I whispered to him.

"No, she hasn't told me, but I had suspicions that her decor has definitely given away."

"Decor?" I asked as I stepped from the foyer to the living room.

My living room was filled with silver and white balloons, as in every single wall had some sort of balloon arch adorning it. There was also some expertly draped gauze and flickering candles underneath said gauze. I took a moment to confirm they were those electric tea lights and that Lola had not planned to burn down my home for the sake of aesthetics. On my coffee table, a Costco cake with an outline of a ghost piped on it and a pitcher of margaritas were arranged. In the center of this sat my parents on my laptop screen.

"How did you know my password?" I asked Lola as I sat down.

"Everyone knows your password," Lola, Bruce, and my parents responded back as if on cue.

"Honey, what is this news that Lola said you needed to share? You're not sick are you? On our last few calls you've seemed off." My mother had immediately taken control of our meeting. My dad sat stoically beside her. He was the definition of the strong and silent type.

"No point in beating around the bush," I paused, took a deep breath, and then let it out as quickly as possible. "I currently hold the death reader mantle and as of tomorrow, due to an arbitration with the previous death mantle holder's family, I will be exposed and likely some people might try to kill me to get the powers. Now that I think about it, they may try and get to me through you, so you should really tell my sister. Also, people may begin to ask you to have me reach out to deceased loved ones. Please do not make any commitments on my behalf." I plopped down on the couch and pulled the computer onto my lap, and then I used my index and middle finger to point at my own eyes and then my mother's on the screen. "I'm looking at you, Mom."

My mom didn't miss a beat. "Well, if people are looking for closure, and you have a this coveted power, I don't know why you wouldn't want to help people."

I let out a dramatic sigh and sank back into the cushions while mad dogging Lola for setting me up.

"Mom, you know I like to help people, but not everyone that dies stays on this plane. The ones I have met are…" I paused to give myself time to think of the nicest way to say sociopaths and oddballs, "interesting characters."

My mom opened her mouth to speak, but my father held his hand up. My father usually just towered over my mom silently, so this was new. He aimed to maintain a single facial expression at most times. That facial expression was indifferent or possibly "sick of your shit," depending on who you asked. But now, the corners of his eyes creased with concern.

"Your mother will not be volunteering your services because she will not be advertising them."

"Well, I didn't plan on advertising them. Peg just said the news was going to come out tomorrow. There is nothing we can do about that."

My dad nodded. "Nobody in their right mind would want to become the family therapist between the living and the dead. Enough people are gonna approach her without you booking appointments for her."

My mom's mouth went into a flat line. My parents didn't argue often, and my dad definitely knew better than to tell her what to do. Silence filled the air, and I looked up to see Lola and Bruce awkwardly shifting from one foot to another before Lola pointed to my kitchen and pulled Bruce along behind her.

"You're right, James. I wasn't thinking. This is just happening too fast. I wish you'd told us sooner, Peg."

"I should have, but everything I'd read and heard told me I needed to keep it secret to protect the people I care about." My chest tightened when I saw the hurt in her eyes.

"Secrets don't belong between family," my mom countered.

"Where is that logic when you hide an extra bag of

tamales in the deep freezer and tell me we're out?" My father responded, deadpan.

The tension broke instantly.

"That's different." My mom's tanned skin took on a hint of redness.

"Personally, I think that's worse," I chimed in. Deflection was all I had to offer at this point.

My father gave a nod of solidarity returning to his typical stoic nature.

My mom threw her hands up in the air. "You two are impossible." She set her hands back down and looked at me again. "What can we do to help you?"

"Like I said before, can you tell my sister? I know I should, but, really, this is all happening too fast, and I need to get my head in order before the arbitration tomorrow. She'll be pissed that I didn't call her myself, but let her know that I will call her next week as soon as the dust settles. I have too many balls in the air at the moment to deal with her, too."

"She's not going to like it, but I will tell her to leave you be this week," my mom agreed. "Do you want us to come and stay with you?"

"Eh, now's not really a good time." I thought about the dead goblin in my previous pool, rogue goblins attacking people on the street, or Alice's family somehow finding out about my parents and cornering them on the street.

My mom didn't look convinced.

"Just give me a week to try and get my house in order, and then you guys can come on up." I had no idea what the state of my life would be in a week: it could be better or significantly worse. What I did know was that my parents visiting in the middle of no less than three personal crises was next week's problem.

My mom reluctantly agreed after my father placed his

hand on her shoulder, and I shut down the call. I closed my laptop and flung it on the couch cushion beside me before melting into the cushions and grabbing another pillow to cover my face. I heard Lola and Bruce enter the room.

"I'm not going to smother you, Peg. I don't want to talk ghosts, and with my luck I think the mantle would choose me over Bruce."

I removed the pillow and glared at my best friend.

"Why the ambush?"

"You had to rip the Band-Aid off tonight. I thought it would be easier if I had it set up and ready to go."

She was right, but still.

"Balloon arches?" I asked looking around the room imagining the nightmare of disassembling the decorations.

"I saw it online! Michaels had all of the supplies I needed. Isn't it cute?" She looked around, admiring her own handiwork.

The genuine enthusiasm in her eyes stopped me from what I wanted to say next.

"Well, you two are going to have to drink those margaritas yourselves. I have the arbitration tomorrow, but give me a slice of cake," I demanded.

Bruce immediately began cutting me a generous corner piece.

"We are definitely willing to drink the margaritas," he said and handed me the slice along with a plastic fork. So, that's how my night ended. Gorging myself on cake while two of my closest friends got drunk in my living room and made googly eyes at each other. They hadn't said anything to me yet, but it was obvious that their relationship had changed.

I decided that there were enough things going on at the moment without asking them about their relationship status, so I ate two large slices of cake and after an hour of socialization, I excused myself to take a shower and hit the hay. Lola had my spare key and lived around the corner. They could lock up and make their way over to her place whenever they felt like it.

In bed, I called Deval to remind him to tell his mother about my powers and to tell him about the showdown in Florence. It went to voicemail. Was it weird that I'd really wanted to hear his voice? I left a detailed message and turned off my bedside lamp, setting my phone beside me on the nightstand. My heart jumped into my throat when I heard the ping notifying me of an incoming message. In the dark, I looked at my phone and saw the name I wanted to see. Deval had simply messaged: With Mother now, will inform. See you tomorrow. xx. The "xx" scared me a little but I fell asleep with a goofy smile on my face.

6

The goofy smile from the night before was definitely gone the next morning as I made my way through yet another misleadingly labeled building at the Desert Princess resort in Scottsdale. I'd gotten up early, I'd dressed professionally, I'd had plenty of time to make a run to Dutch Bros for a nice arbitration iced latte, I'd arrived on the grounds with twenty minutes to spare, and now despite the map provided at the check-in desk, I was wandering between buildings getting sweatier by the minute and on the verge of a panic attack.

Finally, I turned down the opposite sidewalk than the one I'd taken earlier and found the building labeled Regal Casitas. A little bit of any oxymoron given the size of said building. I stopped what would have been a long internal dialogue on companies not knowing a culture but using their words to sound "desert-y."

I opened the door with the air-conditioning hitting my sweaty body and instantly taking me from overheated to uncomfortably cold. I looked at my watch. I was two minutes late. Could they decide against you if you were late? I broke into a jog and looked for an elevator as the suite number was 2200 so obviously on the second floor. I found the elevator bank but then bypassed them to take the stairs adding winded to the list of words that could describe me at the moment, right after clammy and over-heated. I knocked on the door at exactly five minutes past.

"Enter," came a stern voice from inside.

I swallowed and opened the door. Inside the Belgarde family sat on a sofa looking put together and pleased as pie. *Yup, this late thing was going to be a problem.*

"I'm so sorry to be late. I left early this morning but got turned around looking for the correct outbuilding." I looked at the woman I presumed to be the arbitrator. Her gray eyes had a flat glass look at odds with chest length black hair blown out in voluminous waves. Her frame was an odd mix of strong and bony and her height was apparent even while she sat one leg crossed over the other, leaning back in the chair with her elbows on the armrests and fingers meeting in the center in a mannerism I would always attribute to Mr. Burns from *The Simpsons*.

"Early was it? Perhaps if you had forgone your morning vice we could have received the respect we deserved this morning. The Belgardes were early. You on the other hand have shown up late with a coffee, no less. If one is going to make others wait for them, the least they could do is to bring enough to share."

I glance down at my half drunk and mostly melted iced latte. *Why hadn't I thrown this in the bin on the way in?* Ugh.

"I do apologize. I was still going to be early even with the coffee run, but again there are a lot of weird outbuild-ings around here..." I mumbled, the last part trailing off before I ended up apologizing for not buying coffee for the women who were essentially trying to sacrifice me for their own gains.

Yvette Sarcona somehow managed to harden her stare further. I meekly sat in the one remaining chair in the room, a spindly number that was as uncomfortable as it looked. I moved around a few times trying to get comfortable but just managed to keep the arbitrator's cold stare on me as I shifted. Finally, I just set the coffee on the carpet next to me since there was no side table, plopped my purse down next to it, and crossed my legs awkwardly, knowing that my right ass cheek would be asleep within five minutes. I looked to arbitrator and gave a weak smile.

"Now that the defendant has made herself comfortable, let us proceed."

I fidgeted in the chair again, and she turned to me eyes narrowing. I immediately froze in place despite being ridiculously uncomfortable. She nodded as though she approved of my discomfort and turned back to Belgarde women.

"What is the case you bring before me today?"

Petunia sat forward obviously the mouthpiece for the family. Once again rocking a blonde football helmet, pink frosted lips, and a shorts matching set that had a tropical print on it today. She didn't look melted. She'd apparently arrived in plenty of time to not have to run between buildings in the extensive parking lot.

"The Belgardes are the originators of the Death Mantle and have been its keepers for centuries."

I raised my hand.

"Why are you raising your hand?" Yvette looked at me.

"Umm, I wanted to point out that it has not been exclusively Belgardes who have held the mantle, your honor?" The last part came out as a question. I really had no idea how I was supposed to address her.

She ignored the question.

"You will have an opportunity to state your defense once the plaintiffs have given theirs. It is quite rude to continue to delay these proceedings."

She didn't give me a chance to speak before turning back to the sisters.

"I'm sorry, ladies, not everyone was brought up correctly."

My mother would have charged that woman if she'd been here, so I was rather glad she wasn't. I managed to keep my decorum and not interrupt anyone again as Petunia told the story of the inception of the death mantle. The proud tradition that she felt honored to carry as she waxed poetic about every member of her family that had carried the mantle. I'd read the stories and accounts in Alice's personal library and knew that some of the Belgardes had been real assholes with the power despite Petunia's version, which made every one of them sound as selfless as the Christian saints. Despite this, I managed to keep my mouth shut and even swallowed back my rage when they once again brought up their plan. To kill me with Reaper and, fingers crossed despite it being my second dose, hope that it wouldn't kill me.

I listened to this, right ass cheek asleep and my needing to pee for nearly two hours before Petunia finally finished her monologue.

"Our family heritage is always meant to pass down to the next generation. There have been times when our legacy has been stolen from us, but it has always returned to the family, as it should. Despite what this imposter would tell you, I would have to say that Adelaide has trained her whole life to take on this role. It would be cruel to deny her the rightful inheritance that is owed to her. You, yourself an arbitrator, hold a family legacy with your title and must understand the importance of tradition within the magical world.

The arbitrator nodded in agreement.

Great.

She looked at her watch.

"We will take a short break. Everyone return to the suite in fifteen minutes."

I stood up and nearly tripped given the numbness in my butt and thigh from sitting in the chair for so long. The first thing I did was run to the restroom I'd spotted on my mad dash to the meeting room. I could have used the restroom in the suite, but I needed space away from these women. Somehow I still hadn't taken a shine to the group after they so cavalierly decided it was my duty to kill myself for them.

I pondered what my next steps would be while simultaneously struggling to undo my belt and pull down the form fitting pants I was wearing. The outdoor jog in the middle of June had left a damp stickiness on my body that did not help me in the effort. The pins and needles of my ass cheek being reawakened along with the relief I had at finally being able to empty my bladder allowed me to let my mind go numb for a minute.

I left the stall and washed my hands. On the far wall of the restroom next to the door was a full-length mirror and I got my first glimpse of myself. There is a certain chalky appearance to a person's face when they wear a full face of make-up, sweat profusely, and then let it dry. My skin had a salty yet shiny cast. Thank gods I'd put my hair in a bun, but extra pieces of hair had come loose from my maintenance and stuck out like misplaced springs at odd angles. The piece de resistance was, of course, my fitted black formal pants and white button up looking as though I'd washed and dried them and then left them in the dryer for a week with a few sweat stains for extra decoration. Oh my gods, I was completely out of my element.

I pulled my phone out of my pocket. I'd turned it off when I'd pulled onto the resort grounds, so I wouldn't forget. My hand began to shake as I pressed the power button. I wasn't sure if it was the caffeine from the iced latte, the lack of food for a few hours, or the looming panic attack I felt tightening in my chest. My phone made the chirpy jingle sound as it turned on, and I took deep breaths in through my nose and out through my nose as I called Pammy.

"She hates me," I said as soon as Pammy answered on the second ring.

"Who hates you?" Pammy didn't miss a beat.

"The arbitrator. I got lost on the resort grounds. The Belgardes were already here. I look like a wrinkled sweaty mess. The arbitrator hasn't let me speak in the two hours we've been arbitrating, and the Belgardes are telling this tale as though I murdered a kitten in a sacrifice to force Alice to pass the powers on to me. And, I showed up with coffee, late. What was I thinking?" I could hear the high pitch my own voice had taken. I hadn't realized that I'd been terrified of taking Reaper for a second time until it became a distinct possibility.

"Sug, that is less than ideal." Pammy sounded concerned causing my heart to start pounding harder in my chest.

"What do I do?" I whispered into the phone.

"You take a deep breath. Splash some water on your face, and you get back in there. You point out to Ms. Sarcona that it would be cruel and unnecessary to have any witch take Reaper for any reason other than imminent death and ask the family to provide any cases of this being ordered in the past. You stress that Alice called you to her home in order to pass the mantle to you, and that you are her chosen heir. The Belgardes want to act like the times that the mantle has passed to outsiders have been blips on the radar. They haven't. Ask for time to prepare a proper defense."

I remained silent.

"Deep breath, in through your nose and out through your mouth," Pammy barked into the phone.

I automatically did what she told me to do and repeated it a few more times.

"Your chest still feel tight?"

"Yes." *How did she know that my chest felt tight?*

"Do some of those stretches where you grab your hands behind your back and pull up. Will the tension to leave your body."

I went back to the sink and set my phone on the counter and did the stretch all while following breathing technique. Then I felt this odd desire from deep within me and let the vibration that Deval taught me out for just a moment. It was as if all tension just evaporated from my body. I picked up the phone just as Carlita threw open the restroom door.

"I knew you were one of them."

"Excuse me?" I responded my phone still to my ear.

"One of them mixed breeds. No way, no how, Alice would have passed on the mantle to someone that wasn't a witch."

"I never said I wasn't," I answered.

"Put me on speaker," Pammy said into my ear. I held the phone out and pressed the speaker button.

"Pammy, you're on speaker."

"No, you did not just say that a Soldier of Fortune was not a witch. I've heard all about you people. Alice was a personal friend of mine, Ms. Belgarde, whichever one of you this is. She did not have nice things to say about your family, and it's no surprise she moved across the country to rid herself of you. That, and don't think I didn't notice that you waited for me to leave town to try and usurp my authority. You say you're the rightful heirs to the death mantle, but you're cowardly trash. Peg, you best be getting back in the room. Whichever bitch this is, you had better stay away from my fortune. I know she doesn't seem intimidating, but she can kick your ass both physically and magically. For fuck's sake, the woman just killed two vampire monarchs on her own. So, back up, bitch. Call me later, Peg." With that, the phone went silent.

Carlita had turned a shade of red under her dark tan that made her look sunburnt.

Despite Pammy's ringing endorsement of my kick assery, I wasn't so sure I could take on the woman before me in a fistfight. So, I just went ahead and stayed silent as I managed to scoot past her to the door. Pammy was right; I could kick her ass magically, but it was a big no-no to get into magical brawls in public. No witches wanted humans involved in their affairs, and I wouldn't have been surprised if Yvette had booked the room without informing anyone that their was a magical arbitration happening.

I made it back to the room without further altercation and managed to maintain the Zen feeling despite my latest confrontation. Sadly, I hadn't been able to splash water on my face, and I felt I still looked like garbage, but it was what it was, so I sat again in my uncomfortable chair and waited for Carlita to return. I made a bit of a show looking at my watch when Carlita returned to the suite three minutes late after the fifteen-minute break. The arbitrator pointedly ignored this.

"I caught her buzzing, and she threatened me!" Carlita

had walked in full of vim and vinegar pointing her gnarled, unmanicured finger at me.

I sat perfectly still in my uncomfortable chair with my back flat against the chair back, my legs crossed, and my hands in my lap.

"I didn't say anything to you. You interrupted a conversation I was having with my boss, Pamela Goodwin, and she requested to be put on speaker. She also didn't threaten you. She was just making you aware that as a Soldier of Fortune, I had earned a reputation as someone who could take care of herself. Now the buzzing, it's a bit of an open secret. Yes, there was a goblin hiding somewhere in the family tree which makes me uniquely qualified for this magical mantle."

"Cross-breeding does not make you qualified." Carlita still had her finger up, and this time I saw spittle escape her mouth."

"Oh, really, are you capable of dispersing spirits before they put you in an unwanted trance? Alice wasn't, so she would have to time her interactions carefully, knowing full well that she could become vulnerable to whomever she was speaking to at a moment's notice. Alice knew about my heritage, and she still chose me." I talked about my combined witch and goblin heritage as though I hadn't been forced into a trance pretty much every day for the past four months until Deval had taught me the buzz less than forty-eight hours ago. They didn't need to know that.

"Sit down, Carlita." The arbitrator's voice boomed through the room.

Carlita looked to her but quickly made her way back to the sofa while I saw Petunia begin to urgently gesture for her to sit down.

"Well, this is an interesting turn of events." Yvette Sarcona began once Carlita sat down sheepishly. "Did you know before that Ms. Darrow had goblin magic along with the witch magic?" She addressed the women.

"We suspected. She has a goblin artifact in her home and is known to be friendly with the goblin royal family." Petunia spoke for the family.

"Interesting," Yvette murmured. "Why did you not disclose this earlier?" She turned to look at me eyes accusatory.

"Ma'am, I have not had an opportunity to speak as of yet, and even if I was I had not planned to disclose this. It's a personal matter. Regardless, the Belgarde family's entire argument is that of family tradition. If I'm given the time, I have no doubt that I can come up with the proof that Belgardes in the past have deliberately passed the mantle to others, including goblins. The mantle was never meant to stay in one family, but to be passed to people who can manage the powers."

I took a breath and continued. "It is dangerous to hold the mantle, and it is typically kept secret. These women have endangered me by even bringing forth this suit, which we all know will now be made public. Beyond that, they want me to risk my life by taking a potion that they know has a chance to kill me. I have also informed them that I have taken Reaper in the past after being exposed to a death curse, which will substantially increase my chances of not being revived this time. This request is not reasonable or even moral." I could have kept going but stopped when I noticed the flat hard stare that Arbitrator Sarcona had leveled at me. So I uncrossed and recrossed my legs on the other side, folded my hands over my knees, and shut my trap.

"I will be the one to decide what is and isn't moral in my proceedings. Your heritage does bring up some questions of authority. You claim your witch heritage above your goblin heritage?"

"I don't know why I would need to choose between the two. Goblins have held the mantle in the past as well as witches. I am a Soldier of Fortune for the Arizona sheriff and Pamela Goodwin does not take issue with my heritage." I full-named Pammy to try to add a level of gravitas.

Yvette did not look impressed, and the Belgardes had moved to the edge of their seats. Well, at least the sisters had. Adelaide remained pushed back against the cushions, looking meek. *Is she even strong enough to handle the mantle?* I felt guilty judging the poor girl as soon as the thought crept into my brain, and I returned my focus to the arbitrator. She did not look happy.

"I don't appreciate you implying that I would somehow be biased against your dual nature," she sniffed at me.

"Maybe you aren't, but that was how it sounded." I wanted to bite my own tongue as soon as the words left my mouth. Historically, I'd avoided conflict, but frankly I was tired. Tired of the daily bigotry that witches faced and after only one day of living as my authentic witch-goblin-death-reader self, I didn't want to experience the bullshit from people that I considered to be like me.

The room sat silent except for the hum of the air conditioning unit struggling to cope with the Arizona heat. I had made eye contact with the arbitrator and was unwilling to break eye contact first. The silence stretched out for an unreasonable amount of time before the arbitrator finally spoke.

"I think it would be best if we took a recess and gave all parties time to gather more evidence of the history of the Death Mantle. The history is not well known, and I fear I do not have the facts to rule on this today." She reached for a phone that she had placed face down on the table next to her and looked at the screen.

I finally blinked my now stinging eyes.

"It's Thursday, and I do so hate arbitrating on the weekends." She said as she swiped on her phone. We will continue this meeting on Monday morning at nine sharp. She looked directly at me as she punctuated the time.

"How are we supposed to provide any evidence of the Death Reader history when this crossbreed has all of our family histories?" Carlita demanded.

I felt my magic rush to my palms at the repeated insult. I'd had it with this family. I flexed my fingers opening and closing my palms. Letting the magic grow and tingle there. I wasn't going to hit her, but she saw the movement, and I noticed that she sat back just a tiny bit. It was enough.

"Unlike the mantle, which Alice chose to give to me despite what these women are saying, no one can deny that Alice's choice to leave me her home and books was not deliberate. She went to her attorney two months before her passing and updated her will. The library is mine but I have not changed anyone's access to it. The Belgardes were not granted access by Alice; otherwise, they would be able to enter the library. I worry that they may destroy or alter documents to fit their own narrative if they are given access."

"You bitch!" Petunia stood this time. Apparently Carlita wasn't the only one with a temper.

Yvette held up her hand, her magic striking out, and Petunia fell back against the cushions.

"We will remain civil," she barked out before returning her attention to me. "I acknowledge it is your property, but I also think your exclusive access to the most comprehensive library gives you an unfair advantage." She glanced back to the women her hand still raised as if to hold the women back.

"What is your name again, child?"

"Adelaide," she said softly, her eyes had gone round with the sudden attention.

The arbitrator looked back at me. "Surely, you do not fear this one?"

"I don't fear any of them, but I do not want to have them unsupervised on my property. How do I know she wouldn't let her aunts in the minute I wasn't there."

"Fine. You will grant Adelaide access any time she wishes to enter the property."

"You want me to be at her beck and call?" I asked incredulous. "I have responsibilities I need to take care of."

"So find her an escort you trust." She made a motion with her hand as though to sweep away my problem. "Adelaide and Ms. Darrow please exchange numbers. As for you two, do not attempt to persuade Adelaide and her escort to let you in. Ms. Darrow is correct with her statement about Alice's will. I had her attorney send me the document before this hearing. There is no wiggle room there. She left the property and the library to Ms. Darrow."

"It wasn't her library to leave!" Carlita shouted once again turning red.

"Unless you have evidence that shows otherwise, I need to look at the facts. Monday, nine sharp, ladies." With that she made another sweeping gesture that said get the hell out of here and we got.

I let the Belgardes exit the room first since I didn't like the idea of three enemies at my back. Given their stiff shoulders, I suspected that they didn't like the idea of one enemy at their backs either.

"Adelaide," I called out before they could power walk away from me.

She paused, hesitant for a moment before she turned around.

"Well, go talk to the bitch," Carlita told her as she and her sister continued on into oppressive heat and parking lot.

Adelaide walked back over to me and pulled out her phone, before mumbling her number to me. I had to ask her to repeat it twice before I was able to get the number in my phone. I sent her a text, so she had my number as well, and I made her open her phone and show me the text. I didn't want the women to give me a fake number and then pretend like I gave them a false number.

"I'm in the middle of a few things at work, but I'm going to see if maybe my friend Bruce wouldn't mind accompanying you when you need to go." I was worried about being caught up in the middle of the goblin war, and Adelaide calling me and then claiming that I had somehow restricted her access. It would be easier if Bruce or Lola could just act as a liaison. I, of course, needed to clear that with him or her first.

"Bruce?" Adelaide asked quietly.

"He's a friend. He's a bear shifter from the Akimel O'odham tribe. He was also a friend of your aunt's, so you should feel comfortable with him."

"Akimel O'odham?" She asked.

"Pima," I clarified. "He's been around awhile," I added letting her know that he was more than a century old in supernatural speak.

She nodded and went to turn away, but I kept talking.

"I need to make sure he's available. If he is, I will have

him text you. Otherwise that's my number, and I will make this work one way or the other." I thought about mentioning the whole goblin war thing but decided the Belgardes didn't need to know about that.

"Okay." Adelaide still spoke super quietly, staring at the asphalt.

"Well, uh, bye then." I said and went the opposite direction of the Belgardes. Honestly I didn't remember where I had parked this morning, so I walked around building after identical building until, finally, twenty minutes later, I saw the shining turquoise beacon that was my Jeep. I climbed into the Jeep as sweaty as I had been when I'd entered the hotel suite this morning. I pulled down the visor and looked in the mirror. My face showed the first signs of a sunburn. All that sweating had annihilated the sunscreen I'd slathered on my skin this morning.

I moved carefully in the Jeep, trying not to let the seatbelt metal locking mechanism touch me because I did not want to get scalded. I put the key in the ignition and turned the engine over. The hot air that blasted out of the vents was not surprising, and I turned the AC down a notch while it cooled down.

I knew from experience that the steering wheel was too hot to touch without a towel to protect my skin for at least a few minutes. I had said hand towels, but I needed to ask Bruce if he would play witch babysitter. I pulled a reusable water bottle that I kept in the Jeep from the center console. The plastic of the bottle was hot, and I drank the hot water inside of it. It had a sort of metallic taste to it given its temperature, but I didn't care. I was thirsty.

Properly hydrated and with the air now running cool, I pulled out my phone. Bruce didn't answer for a very long time, and when he did I heard Lola in the background.

"Don't tell her you're still with me."

"Does she not realize I can hear her?"

"Good afternoon, Peg. No she does not realize you can hear her."

"Well, that's embarrassing." I heard Lola in the background.

"Tell her not to be embarrassed, but that I'm going to grill her about this later."

"Yes, ma'am," Bruce replied and I could hear the smile in his voice. "What can I do for you this fine day?"

"Do you have anything on the books for the next couple of days?"

"Just regular horse care, but my nephew has moved in with me and has been helping with the chores. Why?" Bruce's voice had gotten suspicious but thankfully he was the type of guy who didn't lie to his friends.

"Oh, you know, I'm just kind of busy with an arbitrator thing and a goblin war thing and the arbitrator wants the Belgardes to have access the Alice's library for their own research, and I told her about how it's not their library, and how I think they might steal or alter documents, so she agreed that only the youngest one can go in, and I can escort her or have someone else escort her, and I just don't know if I can be on call right now. I will owe you one." I spoke as quickly as possible hoping that the more information I gave would mean that he wouldn't refuse me.

"So, you're asking me to hang out at a library over the weekend?" He asked.

"I'm so sorry. I don't want to key her to the wards, and you told me that you have access and that you were close to Alice back in the day. Again, I know it's a huge inconvenience to have to drive out there whenever this nut-job family wants access."

"Peg, I'm not going to drive out there every time that girl calls me. I'm going to pick up groceries and stay there over the weekend. My nephew Jimmy can feed my animals, and I can spend the weekend reading old mystery novels, and if I remember correctly Alice has some of the most comfortable reading chairs around." He didn't sound put out at all: he sounded excited!

"This isn't a problem?" I could understand his enthusiasm when he put it that way but it still felt like an imposition. "Lola won't mind?" I added.

"Nope, she has to work this weekend."

"Great. I will text you her number, and I'll let her know that you're officially her escort. Her name is Adelaide, and she's Alice's niece. She's really quiet and timid."

"Adelaide is the daughter of the only brother in the family. He passed away years ago when Adelaide was young. I believe the sisters paid the mother to let them raise her since they had no offspring of their own and thought the mantle needed to be passed within the family." Bruce gave me the backstory.

"Didn't Alice have anything to say about that? I mean she obviously chose not to pass it to her."

"Alice didn't believe it was a familial right. She spoke to too many spirits that knew too many things to second guess when they suggested that the mantle would move in and out of her family. This is what I remember, but I wasn't in regular touch with Alice as she became older."

I wanted to question him further. I knew that Bruce had had a relationship with Alice, but I wasn't sure how serious it was. I decided to not ask the hard-hitting questions at the moment.

"All right, I'm sending that text now."

After I hung up with Bruce and sent him the text, I did the same for Adelaide and requested that she text me back to acknowledge that she had received it. Given the arbitrator's obvious dislike of me, I needed to make sure I had all the receipts. After a minute, my phone made a ping, and I saw that Adelaide had responded with a simple "Confirmed." One less thing to worry about for now.

I tapped the steering wheel tentatively, and it was now just hot instead of scalding. I put on my seat belt and got the hell out of Dodge.

7

I had a million things I needed to do, so what did I do instead? I took a nap. The minute I got home, I planted myself face down in my bed. The dampness of my sweaty clothes had dried in what felt like clothing stiffened with starch spray, but the nice thing about living alone is that no one cared if you were gross. I'd only meant to rest my eyes, but my phone began buzzing on my nightstand, and as I reached for it I looked over to my bedroom window. The sun was beginning to go down.

I groaned. It had to be after seven if the sun was setting. I should have been researching or talking to ghosts or anything but sleeping. I chided myself as I looked at my phone screen. Butterflies fluttered in my stomach as I saw who was calling.

"Deval," I said as I answered the phone trying to sound less groggy than I felt.

"Did I wake you?"

Mission not accomplished. "Yes, but I shouldn't have been sleeping, so I'm happy you did."

"Can I guess you haven't eaten?"

My stomach growled at exactly that moment to remind me that it was running on a large iced latte from that morning. "I haven't, but I should probably go to the library. The arbitrator wants me to offer proof of the mantle's history being passed between different types of supernaturals, not just witches."

"When is your next meeting with the arbitrator?"

"Monday."

"That seems a simple enough task that can easily be accomplished in the next two days. I think your time would be better spent having dinner with me."

I hesitated at just the idea of spending time with Deval. More specifically, him wanting to spend time with me thrilled me. Still, I knew where it would lead. I couldn't keep him at arm's length forever and expect him to wait for me to not be terrified of the idea of a relationship.

Part of the problem was that when I had decided to let him go because of the mantle, I'd been devastated but also relieved that I didn't have to make the decision to be vulnerable. The choice had been taken from me. Now the ache, the longing to have a partner had returned, and I had to grow up and decide if I was brave enough to risk it.

"I'll buy you tequila," he said, a playful tone to his voice.

"Deal." I responded automatically. Just like that, he cut through my manic thoughts.

"Have you ever been to El Gato Negro?" He asked.

"The place that has flamenco dancing on their roof patio?" I asked. I'd heard of it, but normally I couldn't afford it. That's not true; I could afford it occasionally, but it felt a little extravagant for my budget.

"Since we're having tequila, I can grab a cab or rideshare and meet you there in about an hour?"

"No need. I will send a driver. I'd gather you myself,

but I need to debrief with my mother. How long do you need to get ready?"

I stood up and looked at myself in a mirror I had on my wall. I looked like a raccoon after sleeping in my mascara, but knew that I could hustle if it meant dinner faster.

"Give me thirty minutes."

"Done," he responded, "and Peg?"

"Yes?"

"I'm really looking forward tonight."

I felt a little catch in my chest. "Me, too," I murmured before I hung up.

By the time the telltale black SUV pulled up to my house exactly thirty minutes later, I had managed to shave my legs, brush my teeth, tame my hair into another dramatic bun, and put on relatively even-winged eyeliner. I would definitely be telling Lola of this amazing feat at our next get-together. I opened the passenger door to the SUV, and the goblin looked at me, startled.

"Do you mind if I sit up here? The restaurant is kind of far, and I don't want to get car sick."

"Of course, Ms. Darrow. I apologize for not opening the door."

"It's Peg, and don't worry about it. Just don't mind me as I awkwardly try to get in the car without showing my neighbors my underwear," I responded.

He seemed shocked for a brief moment before he started chuckling. Meanwhile I did the ol' step up on the runner, sit your ass down, and swivel with my knees together before buckling my seatbelt.

"Nailed it," I told the goblin driver. "So, what's your name?"

"Theodore, but you may call me Teddy."

"Sounds good. I kinda thought the driver might be Griselda. We're kinda, sorta buddies, but she's annoyed with me right now."

"Oh." The older goblin raised his eyebrows and glanced over at me before returning his eyes to the road.

"Sorry, Teddy, that's probably TMI. I'm a little brain dead today."

"If you wish to get on Griselda's good side, may I suggest a peace offering of doughnuts? They are her weakness." He ignored my TMI comment and gave me the insight I needed.

"I think we're going to get along just fine," I said.

"Well, if you're sticking around, I would hope so," he responded.

A blip of fear tingled inside of me again, but I mentally shook myself and promised myself to give tonight an honest-to-gods try.

Teddy and I bantered back and forth the entire drive. He pulled up to the luxury boutique hotel that housed El Gato Negro, and before I could touch my handle, the valet had opened the door for me.

"Have fun," Teddy called after me as I reversed the knees-together shimmy I'd used to get into the vehicle. I adjusted my skirt slightly as I stood at the entrance to the hotel before going in. I followed the vibrant signs that advised me to take the elevator to the rooftop for flamenco night. I joined a group of rowdy strangers in the elevator, and was a bit relieved to see the doors were mirrored. While they chatted behind me, I once again inspected myself.

I'd decided on a fitted turquoise dress Lola had bought

me a couple of years ago. I'd honestly never worn it. It was somehow fun and sexy at the same time without being trashy. The length hit me right at mid thigh and even though it was sleeveless, it was a thicker strap at the shoulder that crossed in over my chest into a deep v that showed just the right amount of cleavage. I had decided against heels. I didn't normally wear a ton of fitted dresses, and I'd decided a while ago to only wear one thing outside of my comfort zone at a time. So, I'd gone with strappy flat sandals in a cognac gold and added a heavy turquoise cuff I'd bought from a native artist that Bruce was friends with.

Before I could analyze myself further, the elevator doors opened and Deval stood there waiting for me. I froze momentarily when his eyes met mine, and I didn't move until I heard a loud "excuse me" from behind me as my elevator mates started to shuffle around me.

"Sorry," I mumbled as I stepped forward.

Deval smiled at me, and I took a deep breath while looking him over. His dark hair had been pulled back from his face in a braid, and he'd dressed down a bit for me. A denim button-up opened at the collar and paired with a pair of navy slacks and boots. Heat filled my body as I looked at him. Yup, it had been way too long since I'd had sex, let alone a simple make-out sesh.

"Hi!" I said, probably a little too enthusiastically, but he just smiled back and reached for my hand.

"Hi," he said pulling me forward.

I stumbled a little, but his other hand reached out and steadied me at the elbow. I felt my face flush.

"I don't know why I'm so nervous," I said, in for a penny, in for a pound.

"It's because we keep starting and stopping before we get anywhere. It feels like we should be much further along in our relationship than we are. We have a hint of intimacy, we care for one another, but we have yet to actually explore the relationship."

"Plus, the whole plane thing," I murmured in agreement, referencing one of our interactions that had resulted in our planes throwing their magic into the mix, a sort of thumbs up from sentient pockets of magic that I was told meant we would make a good match.

"The whole plane thing, and in my case a very nosy mother, who as a monarch has too many little spies."

"I haven't told my mother about us," admitted Peg.

"Lucky." He laughed. For a brief moment after I'd said it, I'd worried he'd be offended but he wasn't. With that he turned, pulling me along gently beside him as we approached the hostess stand. An elegant young woman manned the ship in a pretty fitted skirt and a silk, shell tank top tucked in to give a slightly billowed effect. Her hair had been pulled back into a loose braid.

"Your girl made it, Deval!" She smiled at me and complimented my dress.

"Did you think I'd been stood up, Gretchen?"

"Of course not." She winked at us and grabbed a couple of menus, and we followed her. The entire roof had lights strung across it, lighting up the night. A bar stood to the right, bronze metal work decorating it and gleaming in the lights. An impressive display of tequila was backlit behind it. Farther on the roof was a simple platform stage perfect for the elegant and powerful flamenco dancers that commanded their way across it now. The stomping of their shoes against the wooden platform along with a solo man playing a fast-paced song on his guitar was mesmerizing. We passed the stage following Gretchen to a C-shaped booth. The booths had been set up in curved rows like a rainbow all facing the stage. Lone stools sat behind the booths for solo stragglers to enjoy a cocktail and the show before them.

We were seated one row back at the end of the row. It was perfect. Still a great view but an illusion of privacy that the other rows hadn't allowed. We scooted into the center of the booth for a better view of the stage, our thighs barely touching. A little shiver ran through me, and I felt goose bumps raise on my skin. Deval placed his hand on my thigh, sending another small shiver into the pit of my stomach. He leaned in to whisper in my ear.

"Is this okay?"

"Yes, I like it." Had to appreciate a man who respected boundaries, but I'd begun to realize that even with my fears of commitment, I wanted all this and whatever mess that came along with it. I leaned into Deval and placed my own hand on his thigh as well. He began making small circle motions with his thumb on the top of my thigh.

Then the server appeared, and we hastily ordered cocktails and some appetizers. My stomach let out a large growl as the waitress walked away. Deval laughed and leaned further back in the booth, taking his hand away from my thigh and placing his arm around my shoulders. It felt good, safe, caring. I laughed with him and leaned back as well keeping my hand on his thigh.

There was an electricity in the air with the lights, the music, the food, the cocktails. We didn't talk much because of the performances happening in front of us, but it was a sated sort of silence. The quiet that comes after you finally just let things be and accept what you want without any of the caveats. There would be time in the future for disagreements, logistics, and insecurities. Tonight, I just wanted to be with Deval, and he just wanted to be with me.

After a couple of hours, I went ahead and made my move.

"Did you want to come back to my place?"

He immediately signaled for the check, and we got out of there. Ted appeared as if by magic to chauffeur us back to my house. I'd been afraid that if we left the rooftop that everyday reality would ruin the magic, but it didn't. We remained quiet in the backseat as a classical guitar played from the speakers at a volume that didn't necessarily allow for small talk. *Smooth, Teddy,* I thought to myself.

We barely made it in my front door before Deval pushed me against the wall. His lips crushed mine possessively before moving to my neck. His hands grabbed my ass, lifting me up against the wall. I reacted immediately wrapping my legs around him. I let out a gasp as his teeth found my earlobe. My hands gripped his shoulders as the sensations kept coming.

"Oh, my gods," I murmured as my magic suddenly rushed into my body. Our planes reached out feeling the connection filling us with the heady vibration of power tickling every nerve. "Bedroom," I said as the sensations continued to build. Deval complied, carrying me, hands still gripping my ass down the hall. He threw me on the bed, and I immediately felt the absence of him. I squirmed to push myself up, so I could take off my dress.

"Don't deny me the pleasure," he said, even as he unbuttoned his own shirt. I thought to tell him that was unfair, but then he was on me again. I felt like a spectator in my own seduction up until then, but I couldn't get enough of him. My hands found his back, letting my fingernails slide up it. Claiming him as his own hand went to my vagina stroking above the tiny fabric triangle. When you date a man centuries old, apparently he had no trouble finding the clit. I let out a moan as he rubbed me in circular motions, and then it was too much. My orgasm washed over me intense and fast and my legs began to shake.

I thought he would let up, but he didn't. Instead, he moved down my body and pushed my skirt up further to my waste. He barely glanced at my underwear before he ripped them off and then his mouth was on me.

"Delicious," he said, voice husky.

"Don't stop," I moaned as my hands gripped his hair.

His tongue just increased pressure, and he pushed one finger inside of me then two, matching the fevered pitch of his tongue. It was almost painful as the second orgasm hit. My nerve endings were all abuzz. I needed time to come back down, but he didn't afford me that luxury, tugging up my dress and pulling it over my head. He was more careful with the bra than he had been with my underpants. I had the briefest random thought in the middle of the best sex of my life of *thank the gods, that's an expensive bra*. It didn't last long as his hand cupped my breasts moving up my body.

His clothed leg sliding between mine, the friction of the rough material of his pants on my sensitive flesh made me shiver as he bent his head down and took my nipple in his mouth.

Wait, why is he still wearing pants? I thought even as I leaned my head back, a slave to the sensation. I shook my head trying to get back just a little control and decided turn about was fair play. I pushed myself up back on my elbows and managed to speak.

"My turn," I said.

He raised his head and smiled at me. There was a wicked twinkle there that I'd never seen. Before I could change my mind, I pushed him back with one hand. If he hadn't been a willing participant, I wouldn't have been able to, but since he was, he backed up and stood by the edge of the bed.

Perfect. I needed to get those pants off of him.

I followed him and stood in front of him pressing our bodies together. Goosebumps raised on my skin as my chest pressed against the cool smoothness of his. I knew that goblins ran cooler than the average person, but I'd never considered the possible erotic sensation before now. I looked up at him as my hands found their way to the button of his pants. Deval dipped his head and our mouths met. This wasn't as intense as before; a sensual restraint had been put in place. The kiss was deep and slow. His hands wound up in my hair, cradling my head as I managed to undo his pants.

The awkward fumble that came with removing another person's pants had me breaking the kiss, but I kept using my mouth as I kneeled down. Using my mouth and tongue to make a path to his dick. I didn't hesitate and took him into my mouth. It was his turn to groan as I dipped my head up and down using my hands to work the base and cup his balls. I did this for a while and could literally feel the tension building as I pulled back and ran the tip of my tongue along the head of his penis.

"Enough!" He barked.

I backed up and looked up. His eyes had gone molten. He grabbed me under the armpits and threw me back on the bed and went to climb on top of me.

"Condom?" I said.

He didn't respond but just reached down to where we'd abandoned his pants and produced the gold foil. He slipped it on and then he was over me. He entered me in a smooth push and magic filled the air. Not metaphorical but literal. Colors splayed through the room and magical sparks filled the air as our souls and magical planes connected, colliding into a crescendo. The earth literally shook as our magic unleashed in unison and for a moment everything went white, the potency of the magic temporarily blinding me.

When we finally came back to earth, we lay side by side as his fingers lazily drew circles on my thigh.

I couldn't think, so I said the first thing that came to mind.

"That was better than I thought it would be." What I'd meant was that was better than I'd thought sex could be, but instead Deval took it as a challenge. We did not sleep for hours.

8

There's a certain kind of good soreness that you wake up to after a night of great sex. Normally, I would have taken a moment to luxuriate in that feeling. Sadly, after feeling the sun on my face through my bedroom window, allowing myself a long stretch and letting out a deep sigh, my moment of contented bliss was cut short.

"Peg," Deval called from somewhere in my house.

I opened my eyes, surprised to find him gone. Instead I found Cheddar about two inches from my face, staring at me. I scrambled back, momentarily startled.

"Miss, you really should go to him."

The voice came from the edge of the bed. This time I jumped or did a kind of bounce on the mattress as my hand flew up to my chest.

"Dear gods, Fred, how long have you been here?" I thought back to last night and felt my own face heating. Were the ghosts voyeurs?

"Just arrived, Miss. Again, you really should go out there."

I went to exit but remembered I was naked.

"Do you think you could maybe turn around, Fred?"

Despite his wispy form I could see his eyebrows meet in confusion.

"Oh, of course, Miss." The ghost turned around. "You should know, however, that even in the land of the living, I did not prefer your particular form."

I paused for the briefest moment before getting out of the bed and grabbing the purple robe I'd worn the other day. I didn't realize before but the robe was a little dusty. I whacked it against the bed frame and hastily slipped it on.

"Peg!" Deval's voice intoned again from what sounded like my backyard.

I began to walk down the hall toward his voice but just a little junior high insecurity irked in my gut, so I turned my head to Fred as I continued to walk.

"What do you mean you don't prefer my particular form?" I didn't know why I cared about a ghost insulting my body, but apparently I did.

"Oh, no, Miss, you are rather lovely. I just prefer the company of men."

"Ohhhh," I mumbled as I picked up the pace down my hallway. *Well, that was embarrassing.*

"Peg!" Deval called again louder.

"I'm coming. I'm coming," I said as I walked through my Arizona room to my backyard. I stepped into intense sunshine, and I covered my eyes as I stepped outside.

"Why are you surveying my new pool?" I asked as I went to stand behind him.

"Why do these things constantly happen to you?" He countered.

"What do you—"

Deval pointed into my pool.

"Gods fucking dammit. Pammy is going to kill me."

There, floating in my pool, face up, eyes open in death was Carlita Belgarde.

"Don't touch anything," I said after I gave myself a moment to stare in utter disbelief.

Deval held his hands up, and I turned to go and retrieve my cell phone. I started to walk to the bedroom but then detoured to the foyer where I had become more intimately acquainted with the wall the night before. Sure enough, there was my purse on the floor where I'd dropped it. I retrieved my phone and let out a sigh of relief. I had twelve percent left.

Pammy's number was now set up as the number one speed dial. *Sorry, Mom.* I hit the button and let it ring as I returned to my yard. Pammy took several rings to answer, and I was back at the pool before she mumbled into the phone.

"You know when you were being constantly bombarded by ghosts I had some peace. I didn't have people getting arbitrated and finding dead bodies in their pool."

"That is correct, but you can now definitely use the plural of body," I told her.

There was a pause. "Are you serious?" Her previously sleepy voice took on an alertness that hadn't been there before.

"Carlita Belgarde is dead in my pool."

"Christ on a crutch, Peg. Do you have an alibi?"

"She does," Deval said loud enough for Pammy to hear him.

"'Bout damn time. Was it good?" She paused for a moment and when I was about to answer continued, "Pretend I didn't say that. I haven't had morning meditation to gather my wits."

"What should I do?"

"I'll tell you what you won't be doing, calling the arbi-trator or the Belgardes."

"Pammy, the Belgardes need to know their family member died."

"And, they will as soon as I cross the Arizona state line. I don't like that the family waited until I left to serve you with papers, but I let it slide, but hell if I'm going to let Sarcona make any decisions in a murder case."

"Why?" I asked. "I know we didn't get off on the right foot, but she has to be at least somewhat fair otherwise why would we as a community allow her to hold judgment over us?"

Deval turned away from me, but I still heard the guffaw that escaped him.

"Don't be naïve, Peg. Nepotism and tradition are powerful things and rarely do they lead to anything good."

"Fine, so avoid them at all cost…" I trailed off when I heard the creaky hinge on the side gate to my yard.

"You have got to be kidding me," I said as, sure enough, the arbitrator, followed by the two remaining Belgardes, stepped into my yard.

"What have you done with my sister, you bitch?" Petunia had been following behind the arbitrator but had skirted around the woman despite her holding her hand up to try and stop her.

"Let's keep this civil." Yvette's voice intoned authority, but that was lost on Petunia when she saw her sister floating in the pool.

My heart ached for her as I saw something break inside the prim and proper woman. She let out a wail and ran to the ladder, and with no thought for her pressed day suit or elaborate hairstyle, she jumped into the pool and clung to the body.

"God, no!" She shook her sister and placed her ear

against her chest. I saw her body tremble when her fear was confirmed. Carlita was dead and had been for hours: there was nothing to be done. She raised her head and looked at me.

Her voice shrill with rage, she screamed, "It wasn't enough to steal our legacy? Will you not stop until we're all dead? Did you kill Alice, too?"

"Of course no—"

Petunia snatched her hand into the air and mumbled something under her breath. My own magic surged to my hands, and as I raised them a ferocious pink cloud of magic filled the air. Before I felt even a taste of Petunia's magic, Yvette was there, raising both hands. A shimmer of a large bubble appeared and as literally just sucked the malevolent magic in the air and it began to shrink. She snapped her fingers and it was gone.

"There will be order!" Yvette stated firmly. "Peg Darrow, you are charged with the murder of Carlita Belgarde. How do you plead?"

I was momentarily dumbfounded. Silence stretched for a couple of seconds in my yard before I heard Pammy's voice coming from the cell phone I still held.

"Put me on speaker, Peg." She told me for the second time in as many days.

I did so and held the phone out.

"It's Pammy," I mumbled.

"Yvette, why are you charging my Soldier of Fortune?"

I almost told Pammy that Yvette rolled her eyes at the question, but it felt like a bit too much of a teacher's pet move.

"The woman who was attempting to reclaim a family power has just been found floating in Ms. Darrow's…" Yvette gave my blow-up pool a looking over, "play pool."

"Take a look at the woman," Pammy demanded through the phone.

All eyes snapped to me. I looked down at my barely together robe and awkwardly tightened it with one hand before reaching up to my hair, which as I suspected was feeling several steps beyond tousled. I grimaced but felt slightly better when Deval moved closer to me and placed his hand on my lower back.

"Does that look like a woman who spent the evening murdering someone?"

They wanted me dead, and now I would die from embarrassment.

"She simply looks unkempt. One could not assume that simply because she appears to have participated in a passionate bout of lovemaking that she did not also murder Carlita," Yvette said.

Kill me now.

"Peg was far too busy to have time to pursue a foe," Deval now added to my defense.

Kill me now and bury me where no one could find me.

"All right, we can stop discussing what I was up to last night. Everyone gets it," I said, my face now a bright red. "I am not guilty."

"Many degenerates engage in coitus after performing violent acts." Yvette was not deterred. "Who else would have motive to harm this woman?"

"How would you expect me to know that? I've met this woman all of three times! I don't know her history or her enemies."

"I think it's pretty clear that you caused this woman harm, and as an arbitrator I must see justice done."

"You would question my word?" Deval's voice was dangerously soft. He looked at Yvette as though she were a bug.

"Stop it, Deval, this is witch business," Pammy barked through my phone.

"Then take care of it," he replied, still eyeing the arbitrator.

"Yvette, you had better not cause an incident in my state. Don't think that we didn't notice you waiting for me to leave the state before sneaking into my house and trying to jam up one of my Soldiers of Fortune."

"I don't answer to you, Pamela," Yvette responded, her tone haughty.

"Maybe not, but if you try this shit without giving Peg time to investigate to clear herself, I will personally find you and kick your ass."

My backyard went silent. I just stood there holding my phone up like an idiot.

"I was always going to give her time to present gathered evidence, Pamela. I do not appreciate you indicating that I have somehow snuck across state lines in order to punish your fortunes."

"It's just really suspicious, if you ask me," Pammy answered back. "But, I will take you at your word. Peg, call BBTT and have Craig pick up the body and give us cause of death as well as looking for any additional evidence. Now that you've had two bodies show up in your yard, you may want to ward it, as I have suggested."

"There was another body here?" Yvette jumped at the new information.

"It was a goblin. Which makes it a goblin matter. Ms. Darrow has already been cleared for the incident," Deval said before Yvette could go on any further.

My phone let out a chirp and the screen faded, letting me know that it was about to die.

"Pammy, my battery is almost out. I need to go inside to plug it in to call the Boil Boil Toil and Trouble Lab." I listed out the acronym since we had out-of-towners present. "Did you need to say anything else?"

"Don't try me, Yvette; you may come from a long line of arbitrators, but I come from a long line of petty women. I usually manage to hold in that part of me. Don't make me let it loose on you."

"Don't threaten me, Pamela. I won't do anything until we have more information. If you want to maintain control of your territory, it would be best if you didn't leave it to be taken over by anyone who happened by."

"We're witches, Yvette, not vampires." Pammy said just as my phone died. We all caught her meaning though. Yvette was acting like a sneaky predator trying to control a situation in a moment of weakness. It was quite the burn by witch standards. I looked around to see if anyone else had reacted but was met with a bunch of stony faces. *Right, dead body in the pool. Lost a loved one.*

"Well, I need to charge my phone and call BBTT. Feel free to see yourselves out."

"I'm not leaving my sister, bitch," Petunia said from the pool, still clinging to her dead sister's body.

"You can stay until BBTT comes to pick her up," I conceded.

"I will remain as well to supervise the evidence collecting," Yvette announced.

Only Adelaide remained silent. She still stood by the side gate entrance as though she was part of the foliage, silent, but rocking slightly in the barely there wind.

I turned and Deval turned with me.

"Can you keep an eye on things while I call BBTT and change?"

"Whatever you desire," he responded.

It was pretty cool that a prince of the goblins was

willing to babysit a dead body and a small passel of witches for me.

"Miss, I have news of the goblins," Fred said as soon as I entered the house.

I nearly jumped because he had startled me and the temperature drop from triple digits to frigid cold was shocking. "Great, and I can't wait to hear it once there isn't a body in my pool."

9

_____

Craig showed up with his coworker Dwayne about forty minutes later. Craig was the younger of the duo. Dwayne was the older strong and silent type who communicated in single syllables and grunts for the most part. They made an odd pair. Craig's extroverted ways came off as obnoxious and somewhat gave the impression that he was in charge of the duo although I did not know that to be the actual case.

I'd answered the door and sent the men to the back to deal with the body. I trusted them to not necessarily be on my side but to be on Pammy's, and they knew that this job had come through her. I didn't need to go out and antagonize the family further. I would need to speak with them eventually, but I wasn't a monster. So, I let them take over my yard while I pulled out my laptop and opened a notes application.

I felt rusty. I'd just begun to feel confident in my job in February when the mantle had taken over my life. Since then, I'd been too incapacitated to work. Pammy had agreed with me, and I hadn't taken on any Soldier of

Fortune gigs since then. At the beginning of the year that would have pretty much guaranteed that I would lose my house and have to move in with my parents. I'd had savings. The dangerous jobs I'd taken had come with some decent paydays. Much higher than I ever would have made as a teacher, but money runs out fast. Especially when there were days that I couldn't gather the energy to make even the simplest of meals because all of said energy was being sucked out of me by a hoard of ghosts.

Takeout had been my friend, and I was pretty close to dipping into the money that Alice had left me. Even in my worst state, I'd realized that one of the reasons I'd inherited her fortune had been because I would go through periods where it would be impossible to work but then I'd found out what else that money was for. Alice was the Benefactor. By herself, Alice had bankrolled the paychecks of Soldiers of Fortune who took on work for witches who couldn't pay.

It wasn't the best system, but it was what we had, and I'd definitely been too debilitated to try to change it. Back in my own head once again, I realized that there were some changes I'd like to push for, but for now I just needed to find Carlita's killer, convince the arbitrator that I had been Alice's rightful chosen heir, oh, and assist with the goblin war. No big deal, just back to kicking ass and taking names.

Deval entered my living room, and I felt myself blush despite my plans to kick ass and take names just moments before.

Not your fault. You just remembered that trick he does with his tongue, I told myself.

He walked over to where I'd set myself up on my couch with my legs stretched out along it, laptop on my lap. He bent down and kissed me, and then he did the most romantic thing and handed me a large iced latte. It said a lot about the sex on wheels the man was that I hadn't narrowed in on the drink before.

"How did you get this?" I asked in awe. "I thought you were monitoring the Belgardes?"

"I have people," he said and smiled.

I scooted my legs to make room on the couch and patted the cushion. He sat down, and I unceremoniously draped my legs across his lap. He looked at me and arched a brow.

"You've seen me naked." I shrugged and took a sip of my latte.

"That I have. I'm sad to see that you've managed to get dressed," he commented.

I'd thrown on a pair of high waisted jeans and a tank top that showed a hint of the bralette underneath. Maybe not my most professional outfit, but frankly everyone involved in this case had already seen me with sex hair in an old robe that had definitely been hanging on the back of my bathroom door, not having been washed for longer than I would care to admit. My curls had been frizzed beyond repair from the, ahem, friction from the night before, so I'd tamed them into a braid. It was definitely a no makeup day. I had shit to do, and I was being indulgent even sitting with Deval for a few minutes.

"Note to self—make sure you're dressed when there are dead bodies in your pool," I said.

"It is odd that a blow-up pool has become the receptacle for every murderous fiend in the county," Deval agreed.

"Oh, I'm sure there are plenty of murderers in the greater Phoenix area and beyond who have never heard of my pool."

"You do know that you must now get rid of this one as

well?" Deval asked. He had just replaced it after taking the one that had held Bill.

"I do, but I'm going to run an aura trace in it first."

"That takes me back." Deval smiled. We had first met when I'd been taking on my biggest case as a fortune at the time. He'd broken into my house, accused me of being a thief, and promptly attempted to hire me once he'd realized his mistake.

"Things have certainly changed since then," I said.

"I had a certain knowledge that we would become more than business associates," he said out of nowhere.

"Uh, that's a little disturbing considering that you slammed my head into my door the first time we met and trussed me up like a Christmas goose."

"Have you ever even seen a trussed goose, Peg?" He countered.

"No, it's just a saying."

"Ah ha. Well, the knowing came after I realized that you were not a murdering, thieving, maniacal witch."

I thought about holding out on him for just a minute longer, but then he took my bare foot in his palm and started massaging the arches.

"Fiiiiine," I said, as I managed to not lean my head back and groan. I liked to think of myself as a practical person and after being single for a decent chunk of time, I'd begun to forget what the benefits of being with someone were. One thing that would have definitely made the nonexistent list would have been massages. Love, loyalty, and companionship were part of it as well, but they may have been listed after the massage entry in my head.

"Do you have any leads?"

"How would I have leads, Deval? We just found the woman in the pool."

"Well, you cannot say that the two bodies ending up in your yard within days of each other is a coincidence."

"Of course not. I am very aware that whoever dropped off Carlita likely knew about Bill. Sadly, since I've personally offended your cousin in the last forty-eight hours, I doubt he's going to be willing to have a chat with me about his people's body disposal methods, or if they told anyone who had a grudge against Carlita."

Deval paused his hand on my foot." You may be able to."

"I think any pretense at the whole cooperating to spy on you was blown when his mercenary spotted me and attempted to fry me in public."

"That is what I wish to speak to you of, Miss," came from behind me.

I was already sitting down, so I didn't jump, but I definitely bounced and in the process jostled my laptop and nearly kicked Deval in the groin. Luckily for him he had fast reflexes and caught my foot.

"Fred, you gotta approach from the front." I scrambled to sit forward on the couch without injuring Deval.

"Sorry, Miss, you had just said to come to you later. The family of Alice has now departed, and I thought this might be an opportune time given your consort being present."

"Consort?" I said out loud before I could put two and two together.

"Whom are you speaking with?" Deval asked mimicking me and leaning forward.

"Fred. He has news about the spy work, but I told him to wait. Now, he wants to debrief me and my consort."

"That's as good a title as any." Deval leaned back into the couch, apparently satisfied with Fred labeling our relationship. "Just mind that you do not consort with other people," he added.

"Is this really how you want to have this conversation?" I asked but decided to go with the flow and cut him off as he opened his mouth to speak. "Never mind, consort is fine, just mind that you don't consort with anyone else either."

"Done," he responded instantly.

Well, that was easy.

"Okay, Fred, what have you and the crew learned?"

"The goblin mercenaries have created their base in the hills of the San Tan Mountains, but it's not centralized. The have procured several homes throughout the hills and rarely gather together."

"How many of these homes were you able to identify?"

"Eight total, three homes in two separate housing developments and two on the outskirts. The HOA does not like our goblin friends. Their vehicles have been stickered on several occasions."

I grimaced.

"What is it?" Deval sat forward concerned.

"Oh, just some of the mercenaries have had their vehicles stickered," I answered remembering that he couldn't hear Fred.

"I do not know what this means, Peg."

"Well, some of the newer HOAs have really strict rules about parking. They put these orange stickers smack dab in the middle of someone's windshield. This happens when someone has parked on the street after a certain time, The stickers are a bitch to get off, and really why would that be your first choice? It obstructs the driver's view, so then the driver spends more time parked on the road with Goo Gone and a razor blade, trying to get the damn thing off."

The dead stare Deval gave me let me know I'd gone on a tangent.

"Sorry, I know this is serious. I'll give you the rundown as soon as Fred has finished telling me what he knows."

I turned my head back to face the patiently waiting Fred and nodded for him to continue.

"They are gathering supplies. They have multiple batches of explosives in their safe houses, and from what I can tell, they plan to do real damage to the Superstition Mountains. I do not know when they plan to do this, but I thought it best to leave the others behind and come and inform you."

"Do you have addresses?"

"I have one, Miss. They've removed the house numbers from the homes and sprayed the numbers on the curb. It was this behavior that allowed me to gather the address of one of the homes."

"How's that?" I asked.

"The only piece of mail I have seen in a mailbox left open by the HOA lackey was a notice of a fine unless they clearly marked their home number."

"Great. I can just give Deval that, and he can go with his people while I stay behind and work on finding Carlita's killer."

Deval leaned forward once more at the mention of actually having usable surveillance.

"I'm afraid you will wish to accompany them," Fred said.

"I don't have time for that," I countered.

"If you are not present how am I to lead his people to all of the locations. These mercenaries are smart, and if you don't round them all up, they will scatter farther apart like the insects they are." Fred emphasized insects and made a motion as if to sniff the air in disdain.

"Fine, I will go," I said, immediately feeling chastised.

"Where are we going, Peg? I do not like the idea of you actively participating in this war. It has thus far been a series of dirty skirmishes that are brutal and bloody."

I let his comment hang in the air for a moment.

"You don't think I'm powerful enough to handle myself, Deval?" My voice was deceptively quiet, and if I had hackles they would be raised.

"Of course I do not think that, but you have no experience in war, and you are much easier to kill than my people." Deval referenced our different life expectancies.

His was the normal thousand plus years of a goblin, and mine was that of a normal human, thanks to a curse placed on witches centuries ago.

"Well, tell that to Bill," I said thinking of his head just floating in my pool days before.

Deval waited for a moment to respond. *That's right buddy: this had better be good.*

"I am not doubting your abilities," he said each word carefully. "But these mercenaries have trained any empathy or sense of fair play out of their psyche. Bill is a prime example of why I would be concerned to have you present. He would not have been an easy kill, and yet they sawed through his throat and left him as a warning to you for your involvement with me. Their one loyalty is to money, and this activity is fun to them."

"I am not trained in traditional war, so I will give you that, but just so you know, I'm not some lightweight, either."

He looked at me, nonplussed.

"I'm just saying look at my history."

I saw his jaw clench. "I'm not sure what you're trying to prove right now. Your track record thus far has been fairly impressive. You have power to spare, a mixed heritage that gives you an advantage, as well as a coveted magical title now, but this has all occurred over a few months. These men have been warring for centuries. I do not have problem with utilizing your impressive skills but in a strategic manner that is not simply placing you in their clutches to be their pawn."

"This always happens," I said.

"What always happens?"

"We argue about whether or not I have the ability to handle the situations in which my job places me."

"I'm not arguing that you don't. I'm asking for you to sometimes listen to my experience," he countered.

"I do, but you hadn't even let me finish telling you what Fred was saying. It's sweet that you want to keep me safe, but if we are going to remain 'consorts,' then I'm going to not have your knee jerk reaction that I'm going to get myself killed every time I'm involved in a tricky situation. Now, what Fred was saying was that your enemies have spread themselves around the San Tan Mountains in various homes, they are stockpiling explosives, and Fred just has the one address, but he can show me the other homes they've taken over."

"Why does Fred only have one address?"

I explained what Fred had told me.

"Why did he not look to the homes to right or left of the other homes to gather the information? These are common evasive maneuvers for scrying witches, not for ghost spies."

I looked over to Fred who looked downright embarrassed at the blunder. I shrugged at him considering that I hadn't thought twice about his earlier explanation.

"I'm sorry, Miss, we did not think. In our prior work, the enemy was not so evasive."

When Mallory had promised me ghost spies, she hadn't said they were experienced.

"It's fine, Fred. We're all learning here." I said, trying to reassure one of the few ghosts I'd met that didn't skeeve me out.

I heard Deval make a pained noise next to me. I didn't look at him but definitely stuck my elbow into his ribs. He didn't get to come around asking for free spies and then be critical when they brought back intel that his own people couldn't gather.

"Go on," I coaxed the obviously embarrassed ghost.

"Yes Miss—"

"You can drop the Miss part. We're all friends here." I told him.

"Yes Mi—I apologize, there is the single address I ascertained, and whereas I should have been able to gather the other homes within those neighborhoods, there are also two properties that are on unmarked streets."

"Ha!" I called out. "He will be better at getting addresses in residential areas in the future, but they've also taken up shop on unmarked streets, too." I had turned to Deval and pointed in his face. He rolled his eyes, and I lowered my hand realizing I was taking this maybe a little too far. "Anywho, I will need to go with you for the reconnaissance portion of this trip to help you and your people locate the mercenaries, but I will leave the warring to you."

"Then we are agreed. Be ready this evening; I must gather my people."

"Uh, sure, I just need to perform my aura trace first."

"Of course." He stood up from the couch and looked at his watch. "We shall reconvene at five. I or one of my trusted people will pick you up."

He bent down and brushed his lips against mine. It was

strange, the familiar gesture that somehow already felt normal.

"Why five," I asked.

"You said you needed time for your witchery, and it is a time of day that will look less conspicuous if we were to drive about neighborhoods because many will be returning from work."

"I'm guessing we shouldn't take my Jeep then, huh?"

"A delightful vehicle, but not one best suited for anonymity," he agreed and exited out my back door.

I closed my laptop a few minutes later and took the path he had taken to see what was still happening in my yard. It looked like everyone had left, but I went to my side gate to double check. Craig and Dwayne were still parked in front of my house and were closing up their van.

Craig waved me down.

"Your man came out and told us not to take the pool. Any reason why?"

I'd wondered why he'd decided to exit through the back rather than the front door. I got the warm fuzzies thinking about him actively thinking of ways to take extra work off my plate.

"I think an aura trace might be a good place for me to start my investigation," I answered Craig.

Dwayne didn't seem particularly interested in our conversation and gave a small nod of his head to me before he climbed into the driver's seat of the van and started it up.

"Anything in particular you want on this one?"

"Cause of death, anything found on the body to be analyzed. In case they didn't tell you, the Belgarde family strongly suspect me of wrongdoing."

He let out a long, high whistle. "They were not subtle

about what they think of you, Peg. Your man told them to shut their pie holes."

"He did not." There was no way Deval had ever uttered, "pie hole" in his life.

"Well, not those exact words, but he definitely told those ladies that they were being ridiculous."

My second time feeling the warm fuzzies in under a minute. A girl could get used to this.

"Okay, well, you can reach out to Pammy or me, but she's still in New Mexico."

"The arbitrator said she would like all evidence presented to her as well."

I nearly said: she's not paying your bill, so she can shove it. Instead, I smiled at him. It felt forced, and the look he gave me in return said it looked forced.

"Of course, but make sure she's just getting the copies. The Arizona sheriff's office will want all of the originals."

"Also, I hear congrats are in order. Exciting stuff having the woo woo holder local."

"Excuse me?"

"You know, death reader stuff, my mama linked me an article on social media announcing your new title. I bet that's pretty cool. Must be nice talking to you grandma and all that."

"Um, it doesn't really work that way," I mumbled. I knew that people were going to find out with the arbitration happening, but this was just weird.

"Well, as you know, I'm a man of science and magic, and I would love to hear more about your experiences. Maybe set up a few tests? No one has studied this sucker in centuries. Did you know even I didn't know that Alice held the mantle?"

"Yeah, I've been told it's best to keep it secret if possible."

"Well, you fucked that up." He laughed but then he saw the look on my face and became somber. "Look, I'm sure this isn't ideal, but it's pretty cool stuff, and I'm serious. I have several articles published in magic journals, and I would love to work with you on this.

"Look, Craig, I respect you and your work, but I'm not sure that's the route I want to go with this thing. If I do decide to test out all the things on the mantle, you're the first guy I'll call."

"That's all I can ask," he said and shoved his hand out. Craig had never shaken hands with me before. I guessed that this was what he considered his best business persona. Historically, I'd been treated to his professional disdain persona. Still, I held out my hand and shook his back.

Craig and Dwayne departed and I turned to go back inside. Fred's transparent figure stood in the middle of the road.

"They're all speaking about it now, Miss. Soon the wolves will be at your door."

10

In the past, when I'd done an aura trace spell, I would first meditate, preferably outdoors in a quiet, aura-free place. I had a cement slab in the back of my yard exclusively for the purpose of centering myself. Now, the problem was the ghosts. They really enjoyed interrupting any meditation I'd attempted in recent months. I briefly considered entering my plane. They couldn't follow me there, and I could use the "battery boost" to my magic, but I just didn't have the time. I decided to wing it.

I gathered the ingredients I would need. The magic I had been using recently really hadn't utilized my potion-making skills as much. Excitement bubbled up inside of me at the prospect of putting this together rather than charging into a fight, magic blazing. Once my items were assembled, I found my spell-work pot and mug at the back of a cabinet. Witches with any sense had cookware and cups specifically designated for their spells, and they were meticulous about purging them of magic after the fact. If witches didn't maintain their equipment, they could easily experience contamination, and depending on what they were brewing, they could end up experiencing a weird magical trip at the least opportune time.

It had been a few months since my last aura trace, and traces weren't something I did regularly, so I went and grabbed a tattered notebook that I kept in my office. I'd had the notebook since high school when I'd finally taken my mother and aunt up on their offer to teach me some our family's spells and then added other ones over the years that would come in handy. Like a lot of witch children, I'd been hesitant to embrace my heritage. That probably had something to do with humans constantly harassing my parents in front of me, often telling us that we should all be burned at the stake on a semi-regular basis. High school changed things. At a time when most teenagers were rebelling against family, I had embraced mine and started to flourish magically as a result.

My tattered notebook brought back memories of those special times. I didn't pull it out often. The majority of the spells and doodles had been committed to memory, but since I was foregoing the meditation portion of my usual ritual, I needed the reassurance of a security blanket object.

It took the better part of the morning to get my mixture just right. One of the key signs was the scent. An aura trace spell was one of the only a handful of recipes that contained no animal or bug bits, and as a result it smelled much more appetizing than the average concoction. Lavender and vanilla were the main notes. I filled up my special potion mug and went out to my yard. The ground around the blow-up pool looked flooded because it had been when they removed the pool water.

I was barefoot, and I walked through the wet grass, mud squishing between my toes before I got to the ladder. Gingerly, I climbed the ladder while holding my mug. It wasn't completely full, so I wasn't as worried about spilling it as I was about dropping the mug outright. I managed to make it into the pool and to my dismay saw that there was still a half-inch of water sitting at the bottom.

There was no helping it. I sighed and sat down cross-legged in the middle of it, instantly soaking the back of my jeans. The day was clear and quiet, and I let a few moments pass making sure that none of my chilly friends planned on approaching me before I drank from the mug. It struck me as odd that after performing the buzz spell that the ghosts had all but disappeared, other than the ones I had contracted for the goblin spying adventures. I'd expected to have to buzz them regularly. I looked up and saw Fred looking at me over the pool edge.

"Fred, remind me to talk to you about the buzzing thing tomorrow." I didn't think we really had time for that today.

"Yes, Miss."

I really needed to get him to stop calling me "Miss." I didn't care about being called Miss as opposed to Ma'am, but I did care about the formality of it.

"Are you going to begin your ritual, Miss?" Fred asked.

I nodded my head and downed the potion. An aura trace acted like a tornado of all of the auras that had inter-acted with whatever object on which I had performed the spell. The pool was only a few days old, which meant that there should have been very little activity attached to it. Auras had a color that represented the vibe of that partic-ular piece of energy.

The wind picked up, whipping strands loose from my braid. The world went silent, and I looked at the wisps of aura before me. There were so few, but I saw one that would fit the bill. Reds or other bright colors often repre-sented passion, and a lot of murders involved that energy.

On the opposite end of that spectrum were the muted colors that lacked any vibrancy. They still held a hint of color, but that color bordered on a muddy gray and lacked warmth. That energy could represent murder as well, but the cold and calculated type.

I reached for a muddy plum wisp and coaxed it toward me. Just as I was about to consume it, my spell went sideways. The sparse bits of aura circling sped up, and the energy I wanted was whipped away in the frenzy. Ghosts wrapped around me at first. I thought it was deliberate, but the spirits screeched in terror as the tornado turned faster and faster. I tried to reach for the vibration but there were too many, and the cold seized up my body, and I was pulled under—stuck in a trance as spirits shrieked around me.

"What on earth are you doing in there? I thought you were dead." There came a voice in the distance.

I was being physically shaken and my arms hurt where hands grasped them.

"Let go of me!" I called out. My magic surged forward in my body. The amount of power I'd unconsciously called to myself bordered on painful. I'd been temporarily blinded by the spirit invasion, and I couldn't recognize the voice with what sounded like a wind tunnel still in my ears. I felt around my hands landing in puddles and managed to get on my hands and knees from the prone position. Every part of my body was tense as I waited for an attack that didn't come.

"Calm down, Peg. I know I was a little short with you when we found Bill, and I thought you had dumped Deval, but I just read on that magic gossip blog that you came into the death mantle. I hear it's a real bitch to handle."

"Griselda?" I called out, feeling around in the pool.

"Of course it's Griselda. Who did you think it is? Oh, my gods, what is happening with your eyes?"

She still sounded like she was yelling at me through a wind tunnel, but I heard the horror in her voice.

"What do you mean what's happening with my eyes?" I reminded myself not to shout. I couldn't hear her, but she could probably hear me just fine.

"They're completely white. Have you gone blind?"

I thought back to some of my first days of researching my new affliction aka the death mantle. If too many spirits passed through you at once, it could temporarily take away your sight. For some of the Death Mantle holders such an occurrence would bring on a vision. I apparently wasn't blessed with that party trick.

"It will go away," I said out loud.

"When?" She called out to me.

I sat back on my haunches and placed my hands on my thighs.

"I have no idea." I tried to remember what the diaries I'd read at Alice's had said.

"Usually three hours for the amount of spirits that passed through you. You have maybe another forty minutes left, Miss."

"Fred says I should look normal in about forty minutes."

"Who the fuck is Fred?" Griselda sounded spooked, and I felt rustling on the liner at the bottom of the pool as she moved about.

"Fred is one of the spirits I requested look for the mercenary army Gregar brought over."

"Oh, uh, nice to meet you," Griselda said.

I could barely hear her this time.

"Tell her likewise, Miss."

"He says "likewise," I parroted. "Look, I'm not going to do the back and forth thing right now. Being this helpless is disconcerting enough."

"You really ought to ward your yard," Griselda told me. "Any scoundrel could have come in and caused you harm."

I gritted my teeth. If one more person told me what I already knew…

"Is Deval here as well or just you, Griselda?"

"Just me. He had to speak with Delmy. He is going to meet us further southeast."

"It's your lucky day then, Griselda. You get to help me find clothes."

"Is that really necessary? We're on a time crunch. "

"Griselda, I like to think of myself as a go with the flow type of person, but after passing out in a puddle, I'm not exactly feeling great about myself at the moment. I am not going to go and hang with a group of goblins looking like someone who just crawled out of a marsh. The white noise in my ears had begun to fade so I heard the irritation in her voice.

"I hate to tell you this, but we might also want to throw some aloe vera on you."

Oh, dear gods, no.

"But I have a base tan," I whimpered. Then it suddenly made sense why it had been so painful when she had shaken me awake earlier.

"I know: you've had a few generations in the desert, Peg, but you're not indigenous. You are not someone blessed with melanin. You're another European mutt whose genetic predisposition made your body more concerned about Rickets disease, meaning if you fall asleep in the sun without sunscreen you're gonna wake up looking like a lobster."

"That bad?"

"Yes, do you have any magical ointments that might help you?" She asked. Her tone just a tad kinder.

"No, I thought I had a base tan. Normally I would have created a batch at the beginning of summer, but I've spent so much time in the pool to escape the ghosts, I thought I had a base tan!" I whined again.

"Yeah, you're gonna need to let that go. Also, you should know better and wear sunscreen. A base tan is a myth. "

"Griselda, I'm not sure if you're aware, but I've had a trying day. I've had a trying six months, if we're being completely honest, but this week really takes the cake. I've found two dead bodies in my yard, been asked to kill myself, so some backwater family can have the death mantle, been accused of murder, and been asked to play spymaster with a bunch of ghosts that I had to bargain with. In fact, I don't even know what the ghost who gathered my spies is going to ask for in return. The one good thing that's happened this week is that I got laid. No, I don't want to talk about it, but I thought you should know." I didn't know why I said that last part but, hey, it had been a shit week, and I wanted to brag about the one thing.

"Get it, girl," Griselda offered weakly.

"Thank you, now help me out of this pool."

"I'm not sure you're going to want me to touch you," she said.

"You really don't wish for her to touch you, Miss."

I gritted my teeth and placed my hands back in the puddle, pushing myself to standing. I held out my arm.

"Just take my hand, Griselda, and take me to the ladder."

She led me to the ladder, and I managed to climb out without her assistance. Getting into the house and into my bedroom followed a similar pattern, except this time I bumped into several doorframes. Tomorrow, I would sport some purple bruises to accompany the sunburn. In my bedroom, I warned Griselda.

"Listen, I'm not normally the type to strip in front of people, but we don't have a lot of time, and I need little help here."

"I'm in the military. We do not let modesty interfere with a mission."

"Perfect."

I instructed her in finding me a pair of loose joggers and a tank top and fresh underwear and a sports bra. She set the clothes on my bed while I sent her off to scour my bathroom for aloe vera. I may not have been smart enough to brew up a batch of magical sun burn relief, but I knew of no Arizonan who didn't have some half-empty aloe vera bottle at the back of a bathroom cabinet left over from another day when mistakes were made.

I managed to dress myself with only stubbing my toes once on a metal bar under my bed that existed purely to torment people. I heard Griselda come back in, and she went straight to business rubbing down my arms and shoulders with the gel. It stung before the cooling effect started to take hold, but I managed not to complain. Thank the gods I'd been wearing jeans and not shorts. She also got down on the ground to get my feet, which were apparently also crispy, and then made me hold out my hand, so I could apply it to my own face, neck, and ears.

"How do I look?" I asked after we were done.

"Like a shiny lobster," she responded.

"Great, now would you mind finding me socks and running shoes?"

"Would you rather have a pair of sandals?" She asked.

"Always, but I don't know if we're going to need to move later, and I'd rather not have to make my escape in flip-flops"

"That is probably wise," she responded.

———

And with that, we were off with Fred in the backseat. The cold air his presence brought felt nice on my abused skin. I'd briefly tried to convince Griselda that an iced latte would probably speed up my eyesight recovery. She didn't buy it and told me we were already late. I didn't pout because I was an adult, although I really wanted a latte. We chitchatted for a bit in the car, mostly about our respective cats.

We both pointedly avoided talking about Deval. For me it was because I was pretty sure that Griselda was the man's BFF, and I'd already admitted to knocking boots with him. Even though my and Deval's relationship felt oddly stable at this exact moment, I worried that I was lying to myself, and it was just one of those whirlwind relationships where it was intense, fast, all consuming, and just as quickly I might either get ghosted or be the ghostee. We'd alternated hitting the gas and the brakes in the past, but right now it felt like the gas pedal was pushed all the way down.

After letting silence stretch for a few minutes, Griselda put me out of my own over-thinking misery and turned on the radio. I don't know what I had been expecting, but the house music that pulsed from the speakers wasn't it. The vibration of the base soothed me, and I rested my head against the window until I felt Griselda pull into a parking lot and stop the car, killing the music simultaneously.

My door was pulled open, and startled, my magic jumped forward and hit the person who'd opened my door with just a small pushback spell.

I heard a grunt.

"What are you doing?" Deval asked. No worse for wear obviously. The thick skin and generally heartier bearing of goblins gave them some immunity to combat witch magic. They still felt it, but to do real damage it needed to be a series of blows.

"Sorry, I didn't know who you were."

"Excuse me?" Deval sounded confused. But then I felt his finger on my chin as he tilted my face up. "What have you done to yourself? I only left you alone for a few hours."

"Her eyes looked a lot creepier an hour ago." Griselda volunteered from the driver's seat.

"A little mishap from the aura trace. I've been told that it should be gone any time now. In fact I'm starting to see shadows again."

I felt his lips brush against mine.

I guess we're not even pretending to keep this a secret.

I was probably blushing, but my skin was already red from the sunburn.

"I will ride with you two."

"Three," I corrected, thinking of Fred in the back.

There was a small pause. *Hey, if you wanted ghost spies then you got ghost ride alongs.*

"Three," Deval agreed. "We have two other cars that will stay outside of the communities as we do our drive-by in an attempt to remain unnoticed. The other vehicles are simply here should we need backup. Is this going to be a problem, Peg?"

"Is what going to a problem?"

"Your temporary blindness," Griselda chimed in for Deval. She was much too formal to say "duh," but I heard it nonetheless.

"Like I said, I'm seeing shadows and light now. Should clear up any minute according to Fred, and as we've already gone over, I am not engaging in war. I'm simply here as the interpreter for Fred."

"Fine. Since you cannot see, I am going to move you to the backseat." Deval grabbed my hand.

"I get car sick." I said on autopilot.

"Does that even happen if you can't see?" Deval asked.

"Well, I guess we're about to find out," I mumbled as I stumbled out f the car. Deval kept me relatively steady, but it still felt awkward. I felt my way along the vehicle to the backdoor and opened it.

"Fred, are you on this side?"

"I will scoot over, Miss." Scoot sounded pretty funny with his upper-crust accent.

Once everyone was settled according to the new seating chart, Griselda started the car again, and I relayed the first address so we would have a starting point to look for the other homes. My vision had steadily begun to sharpen, and I saw the entryway to the subdivision. Iterations of the DeVille housing developments were all over San Tan and Queen Creek. I'd never lived in one, but I'd known people who had.

Apparently the residents were oddly competitive about which variation of the same five floor plans a person had chosen along with which mildly rebranded division they lived in. This first stop was simply "DeVille," meaning it was the first development to go up. The later, more luxurious, divisions looked on this particular neighborhood. I knew this because of an acquaintance who had lived here and had gone over the hierarchy with me, though I'd forgotten the specific details.

I'd relayed the address that Fred gave me and rattled off the instructions he provided as we went along a winding road that sprouted off in a confusing number of directions. My sight had pretty much cleared up by the time Griselda slowed the vehicle to about five MPH below the speed limit in front of a house where someone had spray-painted over the curb number. With my vision cleared, I saw that car we were in had a dark tint on the windows. A good thing as Deval held up his phone. The sound of a picture being captured clicked several times before he lowered his arm and faced forward once more.

Griselda didn't pick up any speed as we passed it despite some yahoo riding her ass only to eventually pass her in an overly aggressive maneuver. I clearly saw the middle finger he held out of the window of his lifted truck. I guess that meant my sight was back. She ignored it, and we continued at about twenty miles an hour.

"Fred, you said there were three houses in two divisions?"

"Yes, Miss. We need to make a turn at the upcoming street."

So it went. Once Deval realized I'd regained my sight, he handed back a notebook and pen that they kept in the glove compartment and had me start writing down the addresses, so the goblins could research them more later. We drove slowly along the labyrinth of side roads that that circled various community areas: parks, pools, clubhouses, one section even had a driving range. The motion sickness I'd mentioned earlier had me particularly hating this mission, but I kept it to myself in the hopes that our trip would soon be over. It wasn't.

We finally finished with the planned communities and

went to scope out the off-the-beaten-path homes Fred had mentioned. We'd returned to the main road, Hunt Highway, to access the unmarked side roads that looked camouflaged, though I didn't think on purpose. A white three-board fence lined the official communities we just left, after driving for a while Fred barked at me pointing to a barely visible dirt road, just after the fence ended. I jumped in my seat and gestured wildly, so that Griselda didn't miss the turn.

The next couple of miles involved traveling on a dirt road, me considering asking Griselda to pull over so I could yak on the side of the road, and a lot of ghost translation. It was getting close to dusk and the cover of rush hour traffic returning home had become sparse, even in the gated areas. In the hills, there were plenty of homes, but each property had an acre of land minimum and most of the unpaved driveways had pickup trucks. Our small sedan, which I assumed was chosen to be inconspicuous, was a little out of place.

Fred pointed to a midsize, boxy house in the distance that had its porch light on, a lone figure standing on its visible deck.

"Fred says that where that guy is standing on the deck is one of the houses."

As we drove by the road, I jotted down the street name, but as Griselda continued on down the road we were on, I didn't get the opportunity to get the exact street address.

"We'll cross reference the roads later," Deval said, answering my unspoken question.

"One more, right, Fred?" I asked. I doubted that anyone could see it under my sunburn, but I'd begun to turn a little green at the gills.

"It is just over this hill, Miss."

We drove by the final home. The last one's boxy

appearance made me suspect a manufactured home with a nice stucco job. The final home was definitely not the same. It was a two-story custom adobe number with inset round windows and professional xeriscaping in the yard to match the surrounding desert. The mailbox out front had once had numbers on it, but they too had been spray-painted black. It wasn't an issue. The crossroads were good enough to go by.

Deval's earlier guess that this had been a counter measure against scrying for a location held water, especially when I examined what they all had in common: the housing development homes, the manufactured home, and even the custom home were all common designs in the Valley of the Sun. None of them would be out of place in a large number of areas throughout the state.

We passed the final home without pausing just as we had the other houses. We'd made it a block when fire filled the sky. Our car shook as an explosion rocked the mountain.

Deval didn't hesitate. "Drop me here, Griselda, and take Peg to safety." He said, already undoing his seatbelt and opening the door of the moving vehicle.

"But—-" Griselda started before I could open my mouth to argue.

"It's an order," he said, without looking back as he melted into the desert.

I reached for my own handle but heard the click. She'd engaged the child locks. *What the fuck.*

Her eyes met mine on the rearview mirror.

"I'm sorry, but I can't disobey a direct order."

"I could help."

She shook her head "no."

"Fred, follow Deval. Return to me at once if he is in grave danger." Just like that, Fred blinked out of the car. I still wasn't sure how the spirits moved in the world, and I really needed to have a conversation with them about that. In the meantime, if Deval wasn't going to allow me to help him in the open then I would do it my way.

"Do you think it is wise to set your spies on him?" Griselda wanted to know.

I unbuckled my seatbelt and began to awkwardly make my way to the front seat despite the tiny space between the front seats and the size of my ass.

"What are you doing?" Griselda began though she stopped talking I reached for her shoulder to balance myself, somehow missed, and grabbed her neck. She jerked to try and get away from me.

"Sorry, sorry! This is not intentional. I just wanna get in the front." I quickly moved my hand to her shoulder.

She lightly swatted at me as I definitely grabbed her a couple more times as I straddled the center console before finally making it into the front seat.

"I do not care that I do not have the ability to lock this door on you. Deval has ordered me to get you out of here."

I set my feet firmly on the floor of the car and reached for the seatbelt.

"I don't plan on jumping out of the car in an attempt to find Deval. He's long gone. As for your second question, yes, I will set the spies he requested that I gather for him, against him. if he's going to act like a jackass."

"But, you will not attempt to escape now?" Griselda held her arm out as though to block me in.

I batted her arm away.

"I don't think I would have put on my seatbelt if I were planning on doing a tuck and roll. Where are we going? Do you know where we're going?" I'd assumed that Griselda would have pulled a U-turn earlier, but it appeared that getting me to safety was more important than a speedy exit plan.

"I know where we're going," she said. Now that I'd all but sworn to her that I'd behave, she gripped the steering wheel with both hands studying the road before us.

"Miss!"

My hand instinctively grabbed the "oh shit bar" as the cabin took on the chill that had been missing since Fred had left.

"Is he in danger?" I demanded.

"No, madam, he spies." Patrice found me. "The other safe house with explosives is set to blow."

"Is he at that safe house?"

"What is happening?" Griselda demanded, her head twisting as she tried to watch the road and interrogate me at the same time.

"I'm trying to find out. Just drive!" I yelled. I didn't mean to yell.

"Where is the second house?" I prodded.

"It was the first house. It could go off at any minute."

"Oh, dear gods," I murmured. My mind went a mile a minute thinking over all of the horrific scenarios.

"What is it?" Griselda reached out and gripped the front of my shirt as though to shake me.

"You need to turn around right now."

"No."

"They're going to blow that first house in the middle of human homes. There are families and children there."

She hesitated.

"You know if there are any signs of magic, witches will end up taking the blame for this. We've never benefited from exposing goblins, and we've taken former friendships seriously. If you allow this to happen, I can't say for sure that our silence would continue."

I let that hang in the air for a moment.

Griselda slowed, but she didn't turn around.

"You're goblin, too."

"I am, but I was a witch first, and it's not my choice. We need to try and save those people. It's the right thing to do."

Griselda released my shirt and made the sharp turn. Gravel and dirt billowed behind us as she raced back down the hill. As she did so, she pulled a phone from the center console.

She hit a button and held it up to her ear.

"They've blown one of their safe houses in the hills. Deval is on the ground. I've been tasked with delivering his package to safety, but she has received new intel and plans have changed. A second location is about to be blown up in a residential area. It could cause an incident."

I could make out a clipped tone but nothing else from the person on the other end.

"I'm headed there now to try and mitigate any magical blowback. The witch has pointed out that her kind would not appreciate being the scapegoat if we are unable to maintain our strength."

Okay, I hadn't said exactly that but whatevs.

We passed the boxy house. Flames engulfed it, but I barely had time to glance at it as we flew past.

"The first explosion took place in the hills behind. Take Hunt Highway east and make the first turn after the fence ends. There is some brush blocking it. You will almost miss the road, but you won't miss the fire."

Another pause.

"What was the address on the house again?"

I went to reach for the notebook I'd left in the backseat when Fred spoke up.

"It was the home we were first able to find the address for: 1267 Saguaro Drive."

I relayed it to Griselda, and she immediately hung up the phone.

"He heard you, the teams are splitting, half will check on our prince, and the other half will join us in an attempt to reign in the slaughter."

"That was a truly horrifying way to put that," I told her.

She didn't answer as she made a sharp left almost fish-tailing the car as the tires went from dirt to asphalt.

11

————

We pulled up behind an SUV across the street from the nondescript two-story stucco home. Six goblins in nondescript clothes rushed out of it. We followed suit. I looked to either side of us, and my stomach dropped. We had made it just in time for the evening walking hour. There were women with strollers, couples walking dogs, and teenagers returning from the park at the end of the road.

"Get these people out of here!" I screamed at the goblins. They immediately jumped into action herding people away from their own homes.

"Fred, how long do we have?"

Patrice's shadowy figure appeared out of nowhere.

"You don't have any time!" She shrieked.

"There is no time!" I yelled. "Move, move! Get under cover!"

Then I saw them out of the corner of my eye. A group of kids had turned from a side street dangerously close to the house. An adorable little girl tottered on a slow moving skateboard. She had on all the safety gear, but three teenage boys trotted beside her with their arms held out to keep her from falling. They were moving straight toward the danger zone.

"Noooooo!" I yelled running toward them.

I heard Griselda yelling behind me, but I didn't have time to stop. I felt the tiniest tremble in the ground, my goblin senses screaming at me that something was wrong. In that moment I had perfect clarity. My magic surged out of me and while it wasn't quite a field, it was energy and it took up space all around me. I jumped in front of the pack of children, falling to my knees with my arms stretched above me. The barely dark sky lit up again in oranges and yellows. It almost looked like any other Arizona sunset, but then fire filled the sky and shrapnel rained down.

Griselda had chased after me and used her own body as a shield for the children. My magic provided some barrier. It was like shooting a gun into water. The shrapnel lost a good bit of its velocity, but it still hurt as it sliced into my skin. My clothes offered very little in the way of protection, and I felt sting after sting.

Just as quickly the world went eerily silent. There was a sharp pain coming from my ears. I reached to touch one of them and when I pulled my hand back I saw blood. Busted eardrums. I stood up and looked down at Griselda. She gingerly moved to stand up. The kids looked to be in shock and sat completely still, but I didn't see any obvious injuries. Griselda looked around us, assessing, looking for the next attack.

I followed suit. Dust had filled the air and had yet to settle, creating a haze in the air. I had a small coughing fit when I took in too deep a breath. I saw people running toward me, and I held up my arms once more, priming my power as I reached into my mind. George was already there, door open, feeding magic to me. My body vibrated with it, and I was about to let it go on the shadowy figures when Griselda tugged at my shirtsleeve and shook her head "no."

The group became clear as they got closer, and I began to lower my arms when I recognized Deval's people. Teddy, who'd driven me to El Negro Gato the night before, appeared and pointed into the distance. The explosion had taken out the streetlights. It wasn't pitch black, but it was hard to see with the air conditions, but I saw them.

Glowing molten eyes moved down the street in a straight line. There had to be at least two rows of them, and they certainly outnumbered us. I looked to our vehicles. They were a mess of tangled metal and didn't look operable. I pivoted to go the other way but there was just another line of goblins approaching from that direction. My heart dropped. How could they possibly have known to ambush us?

I looked to Teddy imploringly, and his response was to turn on the glow. I felt my own eyes responding and lighting up. They had started doing that more often as I used more and more goblin magic. The message was clear: the six of them planned to fight the dozens of mercenaries that walked slowly toward us like jackals, herding us in.

I felt Griselda's hand on my shoulder, and she pointed to the children on the ground, who were now holding one another and trembling in fear. They, no doubt, had no idea what was going on. Griselda wanted me to protect the children. I couldn't hear a thing, but I nodded and said the words out loud.

"I will protect them."

She nodded and turned toward Teddy. The other goblins gathered in a circle, heads together. I didn't know what they were doing, whether they were chanting or strategizing. I looked around frantically, looking for any possible exit strategy I could use to shepherd these kids to safety. A door? A path to a yard? Then it came to me.

Alice's voice rang through my mind as if it were yesterday. I'd opened a door between my magical plane and the library. I didn't know if I could still do that, but I had to try. I ran forward and grabbed Griselda. She moved to strike the crazy person who had grabbed her but stopped just in time, gave me an exasperated look, and pointed again to the children.

"I can't hear you, but can you hear me?"

She nodded. Looking annoyed. Goblins had gotten lucky with all the thick skin and bones attributes. I shook my head to focus again. I might be concussed.

"I can open a door."

"What?" Griselda mouthed at me.

"A door. I can open one, to my plane. We'll have to move quickly to get the kids out the other side before the magic hurts them." Magical planes were not meant for humans.

I think I may have shouted because the encroaching predators began to jog toward us. Panic tried to grab ahold of me, but I didn't let it. I pushed it back. Griselda called over to her people, and they all scooped up a child, ready to run. The teenage boys looked particularly odd being picked up, but they were too scared to fight back.

My connection to my plane had already been open, but George felt my intentions and managed to open it even wider. I'd only created a doorway once, and it had become a permanent fixture. Today I did not want permanent. I was bringing too many people with me and didn't want to accidently invite the Beast's Folly soldiers in. I needed a tunnel that would collapse on itself. I didn't know how to do that and the panic tried to grab hold once more. Then George was there, sending the images I needed to try this.

My magic, the now dual colors of my own green and the death mantle's purple, lit up the sky sparkling with flecks of copper. The mercenaries were sprinting now. They were within a block. I did it without thinking. An eerie, almost sea shanty-like song came to me, and I sang along to the wordless song. I punched into the air and let my magic grab hold of a seam only I could sense.

In that tiny space, the fabric of the here and now moved in on itself. A tiny rip formed at the back, leading to a rocky path. The cloth of reality felt springy, like spandex of all things. We had very little time before the magic snapped back, collapsing on the entrance.

"Go, go, go! Take the children straight out the other side. There are two doors. Either will work." Griselda went through with the little girl followed by the three carrying the teenagers. Two more went through, making that five of the six goblins, leaving just Teddy and me. He tried to be a gentleman and have me go through first.

"Move it! If I go in before you, it will collapse."

He didn't need to be told twice. I slipped through the inky dark hole, right behind him, and none to soon. Fingers tried and grab the back of my shirt but couldn't quite grasp me as the path snapped back.

I had no idea how I'd managed it, but the path I had opened was directly in front of the doorway I'd opened to the library. Steps away. Griselda motioned me forward, frantically gesturing to the top of the stairs.

I'd forgotten about the deadbolt, and the goblins stood trapped at the top of the stairs. I sprinted up them, squeezing past them in the narrow space, and threw open the deadbolt. They all pushed past me once I had opened the door, and I saw at a glance that the little girl's lips were turning blue. I followed behind them into the courtyard of the library and firmly closed the door behind me.

We were safe. Pain that the adrenaline hid flared to life in at what seemed a million stings and aches. Nothing life threatening, I told myself, even as the chills set it and my mind turned to sand.

"Hey, guys, I may have overdone it," I said out loud and promptly passed out.

It felt like someone was stabbing me in the ear. I woke up screaming. At least I thought I was screaming. I still couldn't hear, but everyone had turned to face me. Recognizing said faces stopped me from striking out at Bruce, who was currently pouring something into my ear. I felt sheepish, but it had been a startling way to wake up.

"Sorry, I thought a pencil was being shoved into my ear." The visual that produced horrified me even though I was the one who came up with it.

One of the goblins nodded, and his lips moved, but I still couldn't hear anything.

I lifted my hand and pointed to my ear apologetically.

Bruce then took to upon himself to get right in my face to mouth the word: "DRA-MA-TIC."

I rolled my eyes at him but then pointed to my ear again.

"Will that fix me?"

He held up his hands in a shrugging gesture and pointed to my other ear.

"Great, sharp pain in my head on the off chance that I will be cured," I whined but tipped my head to allow him to pour in the liquid.

I gripped the fabric of the chaise lounge I'd been set

upon and sucked in a breath through gritted teeth when the liquid hit my already abused eardrum. After all that, I still couldn't hear a thing. Bruce gestured for someone to come forward.

An older woman with black hair graying attractively at the roots stepped forward. Up close she looked like a friendly grandmother, if the grandmother was Elvira queen of the night. She was older, but she had the look of someone who looked better with age rather than worse. While I analyzed her appearance, the woman placed her hands on either side of my head and her lips moved in an incantation. At least that's what I thought it was. The insides of my ears warmed, and it was as though warm wax moved inside them like worms. It was all I could do to hold still. She pulled her hands away and the warmth and movement disappeared.

I let out a sigh of relief, and I heard myself.

"Oh, thank gods. I really don't have time to learn alternative communication methods this week," I said. "The children?" I asked next.

Griselda stepped into view then. "We had Bonnie here wipe their memories and warm them up. She's our new witch healer."

"Where are they now?"

"Teddy has borrowed Bruce's truck and will take them back to the neighborhood. The current plan is to place them near their neighborhood in the hopes that once they are found, the explosion will be blamed for their combined state and lack of memory," Griselda answered again.

"Do you think that will work?" I asked, skeptical.

"The people there have already experienced a shock. There is already fear, and I suspect that they will not look a gift horse in the mouth."

"What about all the pedestrians your people chased off?"

"That was unfortunate." Griselda deflated visibly and sat in an upholstered chair next to Bruce and me. "Some of our people may need to relocate for a time."

"Why?"

"There is probably footage somewhere, the blessing and the curse of the modern age. We have yet to find out if there are any casualties. My people and I are ready to move for a decade or two if our images were captured."

"How will you know?" While at the same time wondering if I too would need to consider the option. I pushed that worry aside for the moment.

"We will all know." She began to list of the various possibilities: "The news, social media, sources from various government agencies."

Okay, dumb question. "Anyone hear from Deval?" I changed the subject.

"He has been in contact but is still attempting to track the fiends from the first explosion. He may be radio silent for awhile."

Greeeeat.

I sat up and immediately let out a hiss. Having a significant amount of cuts all over my body while my skin pulled at different angles did not feel good. I looked down at myself, really taking inventory for the first time. I looked like a poorly produced haunted house amusement.

The tank top and joggers that I wore had been shredded as though someone had taken kitchen shears to them to create a tattered look, but instead they just looked busted. Others could definitely see my underwear and sports bra through the cuts. The piece de resistance was, of course, the blood. I looked liked I'd tie dyed my get-up in red.

I looked over to the new healer.

"Bonnie, right?"

"Yes," she smiled and stepped forward once more.

"I'm guessing you did a magical scan. Anything I need to worry about other than looking like a carnival reject?"

"I applied a patch to your eardrums, it should not effect your healing, and the patches will dissolve on their own."

"Thank you for your help," I said giving her a thumbs up.

"Well, I trust you all to see yourselves out when ready, but I need to be going." I told the room in general. I didn't care if they lingered in the library. Alice had always been generous with the space when it came to trusted people, and I didn't plan to do otherwise.

"I will summon a vehicle for you," Griselda told me.

I held up my hand and shook my head.

"No need. I need to rest, and there is one place that is better than all others."

Griselda nodded, comprehension clear in her face. She looked down from the glass windows to the inner courtyard where my door stood suspended.

"Make yourselves at home," I called out behind me and walked stiffly toward the stairs.

"Ms. Darrow?" A goblin called out after me.

I paused at the landing and turned back to see one of the goblins I'd seen fireman carry a teenage skater boy into a collapsing pathway.

"The mercenaries are interested in you." He told me, his face somber. "I don't speak much German, but from what I understood, the leader was calling for your capture."

"I'm sure they just wanted to stop me from helping you guys escape." I tried to reassure him.

"I don't think so. What you can do is pretty extraordinary. What with being able to create escape hatches on the fly; plus, I'm sure they've heard of your recent magical acquisition. I'm pretty sure they wanted to capture you for themselves."

I had no idea how to respond to that, so I went with the classic: "It's nice to be wanted?"

12

The following morning, as soon as I emerged from the chest in my living room that housed George, I saw Cheddar. The sharp twitch of his tail and feline glare suggested he did not appreciate having to subsist on dry kibble rather than his usual evening Fancy Feast. My stomach grumbled audibly.

"You see, dude, you're not the only person that has missed a meal recently," I said, trying to placate him.

He wasn't buying it.

The pocket of my trashed joggers let out a pitiful chirp and buzzed. My phone's battery had survived just long enough to announce its own death as soon as we were out of the plane. George definitely did not have cell phone service. I sighed and stepped out of the goblin safe and closed the lid.

"Give me two seconds," I told Cheddar as I walked down the hall to my bedroom where the better phone charger was.

He didn't like being kept waiting any longer and followed me, taking several opportunities to swipe at my legs. After I plugged in the phone, I sat on the bed. I needed the phone to hit one to two percent battery life to power on.

I looked up to see that Cheddar had stayed in the doorway, tail once again telling me how very displeased he was.

"Listen, dude, you're not the only one that's had a rough night. Back off, or I will skip Fancy Feast for a week." I pointed at him to drill the threat home.

His nose twitched, but he definitely did not look scared.

When I was able to turn on the phone, I saw that I had three voicemails and seven text messages. My phone didn't process missed calls when I was in the goblin plane, but all of the messages would show up eventually. I started with the text messages. Six were from Pammy with several variations of "call me." The tone of them ranged from casual to scary.

The next text was from Deval. A simple *I am on the hunt. Do not worry for me, but watch your back.* I didn't know if he meant he'd found a lead on the Beast's Folly, his cousin, or if he'd come across a wild boar last night. I responded with a "Sounds good." I couldn't get much more lame, but what else did you say to that? I added a second text of "Be careful," for good measure.

He responded with a thumb's up. I was a little surprised that a goblin his age would utilize emojis but took it for the universal "I acknowledge you but am busy, so quit bothering me," that it was.

Next came the voicemails. Pammy really did sound agitated. I almost hung up before getting the last voicemail.

"Peg Darrow, I have something you're going to want to see." There was a long pause on the voicemail. I knew I'd heard the voice before and started to scroll through my mental roll-a-dial when the caller spoke again. "Oh, right, this is Craig from BBTT. Give me a call. I think I have a good trade for you."

What the hell did that mean? I didn't trade with the local witch morgue. They were paid for their services. I'd decided to ignore him for the moment and call Pammy back.

"Bout time, Sug," she said.

I opened my mouth to answer her when my front doorbell rang.

"Hell's bells," I murmured at the interruption.

"Go answer your door. I need to talk to you, but now that you've confirmed that you live, it can wait another fifteen.

"I live," I told her.

She hung up.

I walked to my front door, very aware that I still wore shredded and bloody athleisure wear. This was just who I was now. When company came calling, without calling ahead they shouldn't expect much. I reached out to my wards and sensed no overt murdery vibes before I looked out the peephole. It was Craig.

Huh, I guess he had technically called ahead.

"Greetings," I said as I opened the door. "To what do I owe your unexpected visit?"

"I need to see your hand."

"My hand?" I asked puzzled as I held it out.

He reached into his back pocket and pulled out a cardboard tray that reminded me of something that you would microwave a frozen French bread pizza on, but as the sun hit it I saw there was a shiny substance on it. "Is that slime?"

"It is not slime, and I need to take a cast of your hand for elimination purposes." He said as he took hold of my wrist.

"Elimination of what?"

"There are strangulation marks on Carlita."

"I never touched the body," I told him while he stuck my hand to what I assumed was magical goo. The slime went from a shiny flesh tone to a bright green.

"As I suspected. My putty says otherwise!"

"Excuse me?" I pulled my hand back quickly bringing the putty and cardboard tray with me.

"Hey, hey, hey, that is evidence! You volunteered!" He reached out and pulled the cardboard off my hand snatching it back.

"Why would I volunteer my hand print if to you if I'd strangled a person?"

He'd pulled a plastic evidence bag out of his back pocket and gingerly placed it inside. Then came the sharpie he'd had in a front shirt pocket. He bit the lid and pulled it off. He started to scribble on the plastic.

"You probably didn't realize that I would have instant results, and you wanted a few days to get away," he said, the Sharpie lid he'd pulled off with his teeth hanging precariously between his lips.

"Why are you even looking at me?"

"Dead body was in your pool." He finished writing and capped the marker.

"You knew that yesterday when you took the body. Why didn't you ask for my hand print then?"

"I believed you and the goblin monarch. So sue me. I didn't think he would lie for you, but I guess even princes get stupid when it comes to women."

I didn't roll my eyes, but it was close. "Okay, so what made you change your mind?"

"I found your hair," he said while pointing to my head.

"Craig, let's get real. She was found in my pool. I shed like a mother fucker." I gestured at his own mop. "I'm guessing that even you shed in the shower. Why wouldn't you find my hair on her?"

"It was in her mouth."

"As in you think she bit at my hair while I strangled her? It's just as likely a single hair end up in her mouth as on her person," I pointed out.

"Doesn't matter what I think. What I thought was that I had better mind my Ps and Qs and follow up on this here scientific lead. Does a little hair in the mouth mean that you killed her? Inconclusive. The full handprint wrapped around the dead lady's throat? Not so inconclusive."

"I need time," I told him, crossing my arms.

"I'm not in charge of granting you extra time. I'm in charge of reporting all evidence to the proper authorities."

"Fine," I bargained. "Call Pammy and let her know, but don't tell Yvette yet."

He sucked in air through his teeth and let out a whistle. "I don't know if that would be appropriate, Ms. Darrow. That woman just so happens to be in charge of things at the moment and specifically asked to be copied on all of my findings."

"What do you want?" I asked as it dawned on me that he was looking for something from me.

"I want to learn more about the death mantle. I just want to run a few scientific tests. No one has gotten the opportunity in the centuries we've known of its existence, and I want to publish my study."

Oh, dear gods. "I don't know what you've heard about the mantle, but it's pretty coveted. Letting you publish could bring a lot of danger to my door," I countered.

"Cat's outta the bag, toots. You already got trouble and will continue to have trouble for the rest of your natural life." He didn't pull any punches.

"Well, that's fucking depressing." I felt a little tightness in my chest that I hadn't felt a few moments ago.

He shrugged.

"Well, thank you for being just a well of empathy. Okay, fine, I will allow for one day of, like, participation tests. No lab work, no collecting of anything from my body." I hoped that covered all bases.

"One blood test and a battery of activity based scenarios performed in an afternoon," he countered.

"Craig, you're a witch. You know we don't just give away our blood willy nilly."

He thought about that for a minute. "You can be present for the lab tests I run and dispose of any biological waste after the experiments are concluded."

"You know and I know that I'm about to say "yes." What you don't know is that I won't forget this, and I can hold a grudge." Actually, I was really bad at holding grudges, but he didn't need to know that.

"A burden I will have to bear." He tried to sound nonchalant but he swallowed visibly.

"Alright, but I decide when we do this. I can maybe pencil you in next month. I've been a little busy, and now I have a bunch of ghost favors I'm going to need to perform."

He agreed to my terms and walked down my pathway whistling like a jackass. *Maybe I would hold a grudge.*

I closed my front door and called Pammy back. She didn't answer her phone. She would get back to me when she wanted to, I decided when I considered calling her a second time. Instead I gave Cheddar the Fancy Feast like the pushover I was and took a shower. Great ideas happened in the shower. I took an extra long one, trying to coax my brain into playing Connect the Dots as I thought through my most recent problem.

Carlita had been killed and dumped in my pool. It was a bit too much of a coincidence having two bodies dumped in an aboveground blow-up pool within days of one another. Whoever had dumped the second body had to have known about the first. It couldn't be a coincidence. I needed to talk to Adelaide and Petunia to see if they could help me find a connection between the two.

The question now became: how did I track the two women down?

Out of the shower, it took less effort to track them down than I expected. I reached out to Bruce who was still hanging at the library as Adelaide's escort-slash-babysitter. She had been at the library that morning and had received a call from her distraught aunt that they had not been properly mourning her sister, as Carlita would have wanted. It was then that Adelaide had meekly asked Bruce for a dive bar recommendation, preferably a country one.

There was one place that filled that bill perfectly, and I said the name in unison with Bruce.

"Jolene's Country Corner."

Jolene's was on the corner of what used to be a pretty desolate area in Queen Creek, but the area had really seen a boom in business since the city had built up, starting in the early two thousands. Despite this, it maintained its humble roots. The dirt parking lot remained unpaved but was normally jammed full, at least it was after five. I found that it still had a respectable number of cars in it, at eleven in the morning, on a Saturday.

During the day, the place looked a little more rundown than usual, and that was saying something since it didn't look particularly upkept in the evening either. A cracked vinyl stool sat outside of the entrance, but the bouncer who normally occupied it didn't, so I walked in.

The dingy interior was a bit of a shock given the brightness outside, and it took moment for my vision to adjust.

"You gonna need a menu, hon?" A woman called from behind the bar. I squinted see her. She had shoulder-length, bleached, teased hair, tight jeans, and a white T-shirt that apparently didn't have a deep enough V because someone had definitely taken some scissors to it. Given the lighting and the makeup on the woman, she could have been anywhere from thirty to fifty, but she looked like she liked how she looked, and she had a smile that shined through the dimness.

"I'm good. Just meeting some—people." I'd almost said friends but the place wasn't packed, and I was pretty sure that if I'd called that out, Petunia might try and beat me with one of the pool cues racked in the far corner of the bar.

"Watcha drinking?"

"Diet whatever," I answered and looked around the room. Sure enough, the two ladies I wanted to see were sitting at a corner of the bar. Petunia had her back to me, but there was no way Adelaide had missed me.

I pointed toward them, and the bartender nodded. As I made my way toward them, Adelaide finally acknowledged my presence with a frown and said something to her aunt that had the woman turning quickly to face me. Not too difficult since the bar was lined with swivel stools that matched the one I saw out front.

I reached her just in time to feel some spittle land on my arm as she pointed in my face with a pearly pink mani-cured finger.

"You. You. Biiiitch," she stuttered.

That was all she managed to get out before she kinda flopped forward.

I reached out and grabbed her shoulder, centering her on the barstool.

"Tsaaank you," she slurred and sort of swiveled back to Adelaide, forgetting about me for the moment. Leave it to the South to ingrain manners that deeply.

I stood behind her and pointed down from above her head and mouthed to Adelaide. "Is she okay?"

The niece rolled her eyes but nodded. She came across as less meek today. *Maybe she'd had something to drink, too?*

"I'm sorry to bother you two."

The bartender quietly set my drink on the bar in front of me and quietly moved away, picking up the "this is a private conversation" vibe.

"We don't have anything to say to you," Adelaide said her voice barely loud enough to hear.

"Nothing!" Petunia barked in agreement. A few men playing pool lifted their heads to see what the commotion was about. I just smiled at them and with a closed fist put my thumb to my mouth and poured it back indicating I had a drunk buddy. They nodded and continued.

"That was very rude," Adelaide said, her prim tone was sharp.

"Wut wuz ruuuuude?" Petunia asked.

Adelaide placed her hand on her aunt's knee. "Don't worry about it." She then handed her a glass that I really hoped was water.

"I'm not trying to be rude. I'm trying to do my job and find out who killed your aunt."

"We know it was you." Adelaide responded.

"Yeah, well, I have an alibi," I countered.

"Being the town bike isn't an alibi."

I blinked and took a harder look at the woman in front

of me. I did not expect the heat that was coming from the niece.

"Wouldn't matter even if I were." I didn't rise to the bait of her trying to slut shame me. "I still have an alibi."

"Well, she didn't just die in your pool all by herself." She kept the volume of her voice soft but the underlying hardness remained.

"I don't believe she died at my place at all, but whoever did leave her had to know that some goblins had pulled the same stunt on me a few days previously. It feels like too much of a coincidence."

I couldn't really read her expression in the dim light of the bar. If I didn't know better, I would swear that there was a left-over haze in the air from all the years you could smoke indoors. I held her gaze for a couple of seconds, before she dropped her eyes.

"We just came here to get what is ours. My aunt never hurt anybody, and we don't appreciate you coming here and claiming she did. She may have been protective of her family, but she was a good, law-abiding woman. She brought an arbitrator, not a shotgun, to meet you didn't she?"

Well, that was a pretty lax way to judge someone's goodness, but I wasn't going to argue with her.

"Only thing we ever did bad was the thievin' but them boys didn't need it, diiiid they." Petunia rejoined the conversation with slurred speech.

"What do you mean thieving?" I shifted my focus to Petunia.

She haphazardly spun her stool to face me again, but her niece reached out and grabbed her knee to stop her before she made it all the way around.

"We do need to be going. If you try and stop us, I will call Ms. Sarcona, and you will answer for trying to intimidate me and my aunt at our family's wake," Adelaide told me.

I held my hands up in supplication, and Adelaide helped her aunt up. She swayed a few times for good measure, but I kept my hands off of her as Adelaide awkwardly got her aunt's arm around her own shoulders and walked her out of the bar.

"You settling their tab, hon?" The bartender called as I picked up the Diet RC to take a sip.

"They didn't pay it?" I let out a sigh.

"No ma'am." She shook her head and dropped off the handwritten ticket.

"Figures," I mumbled looking at the tally for five shots of well tequila and two shots of Jack. I reached for my wallet.

13

I stepped outside of Jolene's and headed to the back of the parking lot where I'd left my Jeep. I heard retching from a distance and smirked. Served her right after they'd left me to pay their tab. I looked around the parking lot for the two women but I didn't see them. What I did see was three goblins step out from behind a van.

A van was never a good sign. I wouldn't have been able to tell they were goblins at first sight if they hadn't continued to wear the matching all black outfits. I also recognized one as one of the bodyguards Gregar had with him when he'd come to my house to try and lure me to the dark side.

"What's up, fellas?" I called out to them, maintaining the twenty feet we had between us. I didn't reach for my magic immediately, wanting to see how it would play out.

"We wish to acquire you." Gregar's guy stepped forward to take on the role of leader of the pack. His accent was vaguely Eastern European, possibly German, but I couldn't narrow it down any further. One of Deval's people had said he'd heard the mercenaries speaking German, so that was likely the winner.

"I'm not in the market to be acquired. You won't be using me as a hostage to try to get Delmy to surrender. It wouldn't do you any good. She won't hesitate to sacrifice me for her people." I'm sure she would at least attempt a rescue but one witch half-breed versus all of her people, even I knew that was a no brainer.

The goblin gave me a look filled with derision.

"She's got bigger responsibilities," I reiterated. "Now, Pammy, she's the head of the Arizona witches," I clarified for him in case he didn't know all of the Arizona players. "Pammy doesn't have a ton of money to ransom me to the best of my knowledge, but she will find you and she will kick all your asses." I'd bet on Pammy against pretty much anyone. She was a force of nature.

"We do not fear such a small faction of witches. Yours is a dying breed."

Oof, he went right for the witch feels.

"Cool," I put my hands on my hips. "So glad we had this talk, but again, it's a 'no' from me."

Three against one wasn't ideal, and I started to run through my options mentally. Magically, I might be able to take them on, but I didn't think they would just hold still while I zapped each of them; plus, I knew better than to cause a magical disturbance in such a public space. On the flip side of that coin, I'd been shown time and time again that these particular goblins didn't care about exposure. I didn't know their end game but that didn't come across as particularly smart to me.

"Hey, quick question: why are you guys running around town trying to expose yourselves right and left? There was the guy in Florence, powering up right in the middle of the damn street. There was the attack in the middle of the subdivision. Now, here we are having you threaten me in the middle of a parking lot in broad daylight. Y'all should just come over for a pool party like everyone else."

"We have already enjoyed that hospitality." Their ringleader smiled at me. "Sadly it was not until later that we heard of your newest power. Our leader covets unusual skills, and the death reader is someone he thinks would be a good addition to our ranks. I agree."

"You gonna kill me here to take the mantle or take me back and let your 'chosen' one kill me?"

His smile reminded me of a serial killer mug shot photo I'd seen recently.

"You are one of ours *and* one of theirs. We can keep the mantle in you. You will not go insane, and you have displayed other unique talents."

My face scrunched up. *What?*

"We want to kill as many of Delmy's army as possible, it's good for business to complete our jobs, but your unique magic is a bonus we did not expect. It was a shame that you didn't stay at the first site. We had to detonate the second home to lure you in."

"How on earth could you guess I would come to the second house?" Then it hit me: Patrice. "How were you able to communicate with a ghost? I thought the reason this specific power was at an all time high demand was because no one else can talk to dead people."

"Of course there are other ways, Peg." Adelaide stepped from behind a hatchback. "There are other ways to contact the dead. They're just not particularly easy and often come at a big cost."

"Cost?" I was taken aback at her sudden appearance. Was she with these guys?

She opened her mouth to answer, but one of the three

stooges ran his finger along his neck and made a croaking noise before she could say anything.

"Thank you for the visual," I said, my voice flat. "Okay, well, sorry to hear you wasted a sacrifice on a ghost alliance that didn't work out. Even sorrier to hear that my new buddy Patrice is a traitor."

"Actually, I said I was in it for the adventure. What greater adventure is there than playing a double agent?" Patrice popped into existence next to me, and I felt bumps rise on my right side with the new cool air.

"She has made herself known?" Mr. Eagle-eyed-Goblin glanced at my arm.

"You can't see her?" I countered. "Kind of a waste of a," I ran my own finger across my neck and made a croaking noise.

"You see now why your particular skill set would be valued by my people. You will want for nothing; we simply need you on hand for when we have a task for you," the de facto leader tried to sell the pampered captive idea.

"She is not going off to some secluded mountain range in the middle of Europe to play soothsayer to you and your cronies. That mantle belongs in my family, and you will take her over my dead body."

"Not a problem," came from lackey number one who had pantomimed the throat slitting earlier. He stepped toward Adelaide.

At least she wasn't with the goblins despite wanting to kill me. It was time to see if I could get myself out of this situation. I looked around to see if there were any humans around. In the clear, I sent a punch of magic at the leader twice in quick secession. He stumbled back but remained upright. I went to hit him with another shot when Fred appeared at my side, with my other ghost spies in tow.

"Traitor!" He yelled, one bony ethereal finger pointed at Patrice.

Patrice just shrugged and was gone as quickly as she had appeared.

"We will avenge you, Miss!" And, just like that my ghost buddies swarmed the goblins, but it wasn't just the five of them: more ghosts came, weaving around the three men, creating a spirit vortex.

I assumed the men would shake the earth to scare the ghosts off, but there had been too many ghosts, too fast. The men shrieked in terror, and I realized that the ghosts had actually been kind to me in the past because this went beyond the swarms I'd previously experienced. I could literally see the gray undertones of the goblins' skin deepen into a blue.

"Pull them back!" The leader of the group shrieked as the men lashed out against an enemy they couldn't see.

I looked around again. Adelaide pointed to the men.

"What did you do?" Adelaide demanded.

"I didn't do anything. The ghosts just kind of jumped the goblins."

"Well, you had better get them to stop before someone comes out here."

I studied the men again. If I was able to see past the ghosts, it just kind of looked like they were maybe experiencing a bad trip. *What did someone on bath salts look like?* I wondered. I'd been about to suggest that we just leave them to be tormented by the dead and go about our day, when one of them miraculously managed to get enough wits about him, and I felt a strong vibration in the ground. Just like that, my ghosts were gone

Damn It.

Two of the men had ended up on the ground during

the attack, and they now shakily rose to their feet. Minion number two pointed a shaky finger at me.

"She is a rabid dog: she needs to be put down." He had managed to get both feet under him and lurched forward.

"Touch her, and I will send you to the true death," came a voice I wasn't expecting to hear.

I looked around, and sure enough, there stood Deval. He was still in the same clothes as he had worn the previous night, but now he looked extremely dusty, and he'd acquired an accessory.

"Where did you find a machete?" I asked him.

"Wal-Mart."

"Makes sense," I said.

The mercenary goblins had managed to stagger to their feet.

"You will not be able to hold onto her, Rouge. Too many will covet her powers. Even if we are not the victors, another group will come for her powers."

Deval stepped forward and decapitated the two main talkers with a backwards and forward swing. The third guy made a run for it. I stepped forward with the intent to chase him down, but Deval shook his head at me.

"We need to dispose of the bodies," he said.

"Did you need to decapitate them in the middle of a parking lot?" I asked.

"Yes, yes, I did."

"I didn't think that machetes from Wal-Mart would be that sharp," I commented, walking toward him.

"It took a bit of magic."

"You should teach me sometime," I said as I stopped next to him. We stood side by side surveying the dead bodies.

"Adelaide, I need you to act as a lookout while we load up these bodies." I pointed to the van they had come from behind. "Deval, I think they may have been driving this. Maybe it's best to load them up in their own vehicle?" I asked.

"As long as we move them quickly. We have dallied too long." Deval reached out and opened the unlocked back door of the van.

Adelaide looked for a second like she was going to argue, but instead she threw her hands up in the air and marched over to the entrance of the parking lot.

Any doubt I may have had about whether the vehicle belonged to the Beast's Folly mercenaries vanished when I looked inside the back of the van. A pair of handcuffs were looped through a reinforced metal bar and they'd thrown in a cheap comforter. I assumed the latter was meant to protect the captured person, aka me, from the hard metal floor. *So considerate.* I squinted my eyes and took a closer look.

"Is that Dora the Explorer?" I asked looking at the bedding.

"It was on clearance at Wal-Mart." Deval nodded.

"You looked at clearance bedding while on the way to the machete section?"

"No Peg, These were displayed prominently when I entered the establishment."

"Are you two serious right now? I don't know why I'm even acting like you have the authority to ask me to play lookout when you're both obviously insane. Get a move on!" Adelaide called back to us as she continued to the entrance of the parking lot.

Just like that, the carefree banter ended, and I helped Deval load up the goblin corpses. We split the work. I took the heads, and he took the bodies.

As he closed the van doors, a battered old truck pulled into the parking lot. Adelaide shot us a look that quickly went from panicked to relieved, when she saw that no decapitated corpses remained out in the open. She began to walk toward us and squinted, but then the panicked look returned. She began to gesture wildly at me.

I looked down at the bright red bloodstains on my clothes. The gentleman in the truck noticed it at the same time and came to a stop next to me, rolling down his window.

"Ma'am, do you need medical attention?" The bubba inside the truck had on a Skol Chewing Tobacco hat, and sported an unruly beard and a shirt with cut off sleeves, the latter was not necessarily flattering but looked to be a well-loved. He looked at Deval and narrowed his eyes. I looked over as well and saw that he didn't have even a drop of blood on him.

"Oh, I am just so embarrassed," I said calling the man's attention back to me. "This isn't mine. I was thawing a roast, and when I moved it to the crockpot, I must have gotten some blood on me. In fact I think it's best that I go home before I scare small children." I gave him my best exasperated look and bonked myself on the head in the classic, "Oh, look at me being a silly woman" gesture.

He didn't look convinced and gave Deval another hard look.

"And, he didn't notice it?" he asked.

Deval went to speak, but I spoke before he could.

"Men," I gave Deval a nudge in the ribs with my elbow. The man still didn't look convinced.

"You sure you're okay. You don't need help?" He persisted.

I raised my shirt just a little to show him that I didn't have any gaping wounds.

"Honest, sir, I do appreciate your concern. I had better get home and get changed." I gave him a little ta-ta wave with my fingers and turned to head toward my Jeep. Deval didn't follow me, and the man slowly inched his own pickup forward and pulled into a parking spot. He turned it off but sat there waiting. I appreciated a good Samaritan, but this was really bad timing.

I got in my Jeep and started it. Deval would need to figure things out with the van because I didn't want to linger looking like someone who'd just committed a heinous murder. I pulled my Jeep past the man's truck. From my rearview mirror, I saw that he finally exited his truck. I focused my eyes forward once more and pulled out of the parking lot. I'd driven a couple of miles before I looked down at myself again. *Head injuries really were bloody.*

14

At home, I changed my clothes and texted Deval to meet me at the library after he'd finished with the body disposal. I wanted to hear about what he'd discovered during his desert walk the night before, and I needed to go through Alice's family scrapbooks. Something about Petunia's declaration about being a former thief made me want to dig a little deeper.

A trip through George allowed me to check in with myself and my plane, along with giving the ol' magical powers a boost. I'd begun to feel a little ragged around the edges, not surprising after the last few days. Last night, I'd been too tired to feel anything other than the soothing comfort I would describe as a sensation akin to having a weighted blanket draped over myself in a massage chair while I wore fuzzy socks. Today's boost felt more like taking a tequila shot. Not the after-effects, but that initial jolt when the sting of the liquor hit the back of my throat.

I still felt a little chaotic as I reached the door on the other side of my plane, but sadly chaos didn't tend to cool its tits just because someone had reached a breaking point—

usually the opposite. I entered the courtyard to the library and shut and locked the door behind me before entering the actual building. I knew Bruce would be hanging around but was pleasantly surprised to find Lola present as well.

"Peg, I miss the old days when you were going to be a teacher, quietly grading papers, and we didn't need to worry about weirdos popping in to try to kill you, or dead people ending up in your pool." Not even a greeting from Lola first.

I laughed out loud and even to my own ears, it sounded a little maniacal. When I managed to come up for air I pulled my friend into a hug and patted her on the back. This had started to become a regular routine.

"Me, too, lady, but you gotta admit this is a far more exciting lifestyle."

"Exciting or terrifying?" She asked as she pulled back a little and gripped my shoulders, looking at my face. For a minute I thought she might shake me just a little, but she restrained herself.

"Well, maybe it's not what I had planned, but Lola, we all need to adjust our plans sometimes," I reminded her.

She looked a little embarrassed. "You're right. I don't know why I keep doing this. I just worry."

"Well, I appreciate you, but maybe we can dig into this more deeply later." With that I gave her a kiss on the cheek and pulled away. "So are you keeping Bruce company?" I asked and waggled my eyebrows suggestively.

"You know she is," Bruce said from an armchair in which he had made himself extremely comfortable.

"Any sign of Adelaide, today?" I asked wondering if she had made her way over after I'd left her behind at the Jolene's parking lot.

"I've been meaning to call you. She's only made two

appearances, and the first time I had to shoo her out when she tried to break into Alice's private office. She was here again this morning before her aunt called her to go day drinking, as you already know."

"What do you mean she tried to break into Alice's office?"

"She came by, looked through some items in the library while I read a damn good mystery I had found. I may have lost track of her for a bit, but then I heard some noises from down the hall. Sure enough, the girl was trying to bust the lock using a butter knife she had found in the kitchen."

"That door is magically locked. Why would she try to force it?"

"That girl doesn't have all her eggs in her Easter basket," he suggested.

"She's odd. I've always thought of her as a bit of a quiet people pleaser to the point of being a pushover. Today I saw a different side of her." I gave them the rundown of my exciting adventure at Jolene's.

Lola even managed to not look horrified.

"I hadn't been as close with Alice in recent years," Bruce volunteered. He'd hinted at a possible romantic relationship from decades ago, but I'd never pried. "But, we were still friendly, and she did tell me a bit about her niece's upbringing. Did you know that her sisters bought the girl from the father's widow?"

"What do you mean 'bought'?"

"Just that. The sisters had a brother. Can't remember his name, but he died young. Cancer, I think, and the wife struggled to provide for herself and the girl. The sisters offered to take her off her hands and raise her. She said no until they offered her a big payout."

"I wasn't under the impression that the sisters had enough money to offer a big payout."

"They're schemers according to Alice. She didn't go into much detail, protective of her family, but there was some definite alluding to a grifter lifestyle."

"That's actually why I'm here. I wanted to look at Alice's personal papers. I know I saw some family scrapbooks in her office, and I want to see if there's any documentation about their pasts. I need to get some evidence before Craig has to reach out to the arbitrator with the new evidence."

"What new evidence?" They asked in unison.

Crap, I'd left out that part. I gave them my other rundown from the morning about Craig blackmailing me.

"Did you do it?" Lola asked and then immediately blushed. "Like did you do it to protect yourself? I don't think you're a cold blooded murderer."

"Thank you for the vote of confidence," I gave Lola an exasperated look. "If I killed her I would have obviously asked you to help me dispose of the body, not left it in my pool."

"You're right," she agreed solemnly. "What was I thinking?"

"What I don't know is how my hand prints ended up on the Carlita's throat. I didn't know her well enough to figure out why anyone would want to kill her besides me. Also, it wouldn't make sense for me to kill just one of them: I would need to take out both sisters at a bare minimum. I'd have probably left the niece alone, before today. After this morning, I think if I were going to do away with the Belgardes, I would need to make sure that all of them croaked." I paused. "Purely hypothetical conversation here."

Lola looked mildly concerned, but Bruce laughed.

Two hours later, papers surrounded Lola and me. I'd taken over the desk and had spread out the multitude of folders and journals I'd found. Lola was on the floor looking through scrapbook after scrapbook of newspaper clippings that Alice had kept. I'd seen the books and boxes of articles in the past but hadn't paid them much attention since I'd always been looking for the history of the death mantle itself and not their personal family history.

"Eureka!" Lola called out pushing herself up from her stomach and waving a yellowed newspaper in the air.

"What?" I asked.

"The sisters were thieves for decades. They even got punished for it by an arbitrator!"

"Interesting, anything specific mentioned that could help me besides their apparent history with the arbitrators?"

"It's how they did it." Lola stood up all the way and placed the paper in front of me jabbing at the article in question with her finger. "Biometrics!"

"What?"

"You know, scanning. They were apparently quite good at breaking into places that had the latest top-notch security measures in place. In the seventies and eighties, that was hand scanning among other things."

"Okay," I said, grabbing the newspaper. I looked in the top corner to get the name of the paper. *Spells Express*. I hadn't seen the name or the newspaper in years. I looked at the upper corner of the page and saw the paper was dated in 1985. The article wasn't on the front page, but it did headline the crime section.

Sisters Caught Defrauding Humans out of Thousands

*Two sisters from the prominent Belgarde family have been caught
using their particular brand of magic for ill.*

I read through the article about the undercover work that had gone into catching Petunia and Carlita after a series of large heists. Higher-up executives in several banks and jewelry stores where the robberies had taken place had been accused of stealing from their own organizations. All of the robberies had occurred at organizations with biometric hand scanning, but there hadn't been any indicators that the machines had been tampered with.

A savvy human security expert started to notice a pattern. All of the companies had been vocally anti-witch. This wasn't unusual, but given their stance, it was also a strong indicator that these companies had not taken measures to protect themselves from magical attacks because that would have meant hiring witches. That would have been at odds with their public statements.

The human security expert who noted the pattern had contacted the organizations, and told them he could find the actual thieves if they agreed to pay him a hefty sum and agreed to let him bring in a magical consultant, aka a witch. It had taken months of work, but it finally came to light that the biometric machines had been fooled by magical clones of hands that had access to the vaults.

A sting was set up where several CEOs made some rather defamatory statements about witches publicly. All a regular occurrence, but these companies were then provided with magical monitoring. They didn't even need that. The sisters were caught after hiding in a restroom until after closing with what was a presumably a "don't look here spell" and waltzed right to the safe of the organization. As was suspected, Carlita's right hand did not look like it belonged to her. It was very masculine and significantly larger than her left. The palm print was an exact match of the CEOs.

The arbitrator was brought in because the local witch sheriff was ill at the time and didn't want to deal with the blowback. It wasn't Yvette but her father who came and sentenced the witches. They had to pay back the stolen funds and show how they'd managed to fool the machines. Plus, they spent five years in a witch prison.

Holding a witch captive was a bit of a last resort for our people as we didn't have the funds or the numbers to hold witches in every city let alone every state. There were however, a handful of jails located throughout the country, but there was only one witch prison, and it was, of course, in Texas.

"They must not have given back all the money," I said looking up from the article.

"Why do you think that?"

"How else would they be able to pay a big lump payment to buy Adelaide from her mother after her father died?"

"I don't know, but did you get to the part at the bottom that talks about how the sisters carry a rare witch gene that allows them to transform themselves with just a bit of the person they're transforming to?" Lola asked.

"Their whole selves?" I looked back down to the article.

"I don't know, but even with the just the bits they were able to get away with a lot."

"They did this for years. They definitely had to have had some money stashed, plus I doubt that every victim came forward," I said again.

"Of course not," Lola agreed. "So what does this mean?"

"It means that we've got a very good case to argue that I didn't kill Carlita."

"That family has a lot of issues."

"Yup," I agreed as I pulled out my phone and dialed Craig's number.

"BBTT, Craig speaking."

"Go ahead and send the report over to the arbitrator, and would you mind texting me her number while you're at it?" I realized in that moment that I didn't have Yvette's contact info.

"You turning yourself in?" He asked sounding mildly confused.

"Nope, you'll get your tests out of me yet, but, frankly, I wish I'd waited an afternoon before agreeing to your blackmail."

"Thems is the breaks of being good for your word, eh?"

"Unfortunately," I agreed and hung up on him.

15

I found a copy of the article online in an archive for the now-defunct newspaper when we realized the article was too large to scan with our phones without becoming too grainy to read and emailed it to the address the arbitrator texted me. Finally emerging from the office, we found Deval, significantly less dusty than earlier, and Bruce sitting by a fire.

"Guys, it's like hundred degree outside," I pointed out.

"It's nice to have a fire. Between the air conditioning and the adobe walls there's always a chill in the air around here," Bruce informed me.

I decided not to point out to him that I was the one paying for the AC these days because really the money had come out of the funds left for the upkeep of the library, and because he'd been staying here at my bequest for a few days and a charge of zero dollars.

"Did you get it taken care of?" I asked looking at Deval.

"If you mean did I dispose of the riffraff after you were saved by the gentleman in the truck from my obviously abhorrent abuse, then 'yes.' No one will find the van or the corpses. Well, we are sending their heads to their leaders, but that is just common courtesy."

The look on my face must have betrayed my mild horror.

"Peg, this is war. They would have kidnapped you, and even between my mother and me, there is no guarantee that we would have been able to free you even in the next century. The Beast's Folly have many secret outposts throughout Europe and a reputation for ruthlessness. They are wily."

"Like the coyote?" I asked before I could stop myself.

"As in my coyote, or as in the one that belongs to Warner Brothers?" Bruce piped in.

"Is the coyote lore specific to the Akimel O'odham?" Lola asked. She went and sat on the armrest of the chair he sat in, and it wasn't lost to any of us when we saw his hand snake around her side and pinch her waist before she swatted at his hand. I briefly debated following suit, but felt a little awkward, so instead I sat in another armchair next to Deval. He reached out his hand and snagged my own. I let him.

"The trickster is in many of the First Peoples' lore."

"Well, I had not been referencing either though I would say the Trickster god would be a much more apt comparison than any reference to a cartoon that cannot manage to evade an overly stimulated bird." While he said this, Deval ran his thumb in circles over the palm of my hand.

"Did you two find anything interesting?" Bruce asked.

Lola and I went on to explain our great discovery while they listened.

"That's good news, right?" Bruce asked.

"I hope so, but I really don't know how the arbitrator

thinks. Will Yvette take this as proof that the Belgardes killed one of their own? Petunia had looked genuinely shell-shocked by her sister's death, and what could they possibly gain by killing her?"

"You said they both insisted that the mantle would pass to Adelaide?" Deval asked.

"Yes, it's been clear from the start that Adelaide is seen as the intended heir. Before today, I didn't really think she had the constitution for it."

"She did have a strong spirit, but if she is meek when she is among her aunts perhaps it is because she has been cowed by them. They obviously want the power in the family, but they are not the best vessels for the powers," Deval said.

"I think we can all agree that being part goblin has definitely improved my quality of life these past few days. But I have to say, Adelaide may be better at actually working with the ghosts. One of my ghost spies has already betrayed me. She was the one who warned us about the second explosive device and led us into that trap."

Deval's thumb paused and he turned to look at me. "How did you discover this?"

"The goblins at Jolene's told me, and then she just blipped right in to confirm. I've been doing so much research on the death mantle. Apparently anyone can have a conversation with a friendly neighborhood ghost through sacrifice."

"That's right, Miss." Fred popped in and stood right behind Bruce.

My hand flew to my chest, and Deval jumped up, ready for action. Bruce remained seated, although I saw his hand tighten around Lola as she went to stand herself.

"I'm feeling a cold front, Peg. Is one of your buddies

here to borrow a cup of sugar?" Bruce asked completely unfazed.

"Is it the traitor?" Deval added.

"Nope, to the best of my knowledge, Fred is not a traitor. That was Patrice."

"Yes, Miss, I am not a sneaky one. If I wish to cause you harm, I will be direct about it," Fred told me with a serious face.

"I appreciate that."

"Appreciate what?" My trio of non-ghost whisperers asked in unison.

"Fred has informed me that if he were to betray me he would do it openly."

Deval took his seat and recaptured my hand.

"I've heard of Patrice," Bruce said then.

"And?" I prompted.

"Alice had some problems with her. She's not the worst of them, but she gets bored easily and likes to shake things up."

"She's the only one of my spies that didn't have a quid pro quo request for the spying."

"Never trust that, Peg. The spirits have stayed behind for a reason. The best way to suss out those that would do you harm is to not ask for anything without promising something in return."

I thought back to Mallory. The ghost that had introduced me to my gang, and the fact that she had disappeared without requesting anything of me. That did not bode well.

"I'm sorry, Miss, I truly thought that, given her nature, Patrice was simply looking for an adventure. How was I to know that she would be called by nefarious means and offered an even more exciting adventure?"

"It's fine, Fred. I didn't feel right about it at the time, and I should have known to go with my gut." That didn't mean I wouldn't be grilling him about Mallory in the very near future. "Everyone, please remind me to take up needlepointing and to stitch a pillow to be passed down from generation to generation of death readers that informs them never to take a ghost's offer of a favor without a bargained payment," I said to the room as a whole.

Fred looked mildly put upon, but that was fine.

We heard a creaking on the stairs, and this time all four of us jumped up until we saw the top of Pammy's corn-rowed head come into view.

"Ain't nobody gonna tell you to waste your money on another craft item you're going to let rot in some drawer," she said as she cleared the steps and stood on the landing. "Look, Delmy, the Scooby gang is all here, and I told you they were a thing: he's holding her hand."

Delmy, Queen of the Southwest Goblins stepped up to stand beside Pammy. I don't know why, but I felt a strong desire to drop my hand when her eyes latched on to my hand in Deval's. He probably sensed this as his grip tightened on mine, not in a restrictive way but in an "I've finally caught you" endearing sort of way. It was only because he'd left that little bit of wiggle room that I didn't follow my base instincts and yank back my hand.

"I see that you were right, Pammy. It's not as though I had a problem with the pairing, but you know she's certainly made him chase her."

"It's not worth much if it's easy to come by," Pammy said.

"I don't know about that, Pammy: I think easy love is underrated. The constant drama and hemming and hawing can so exhaust one before the fun even begins."

Then the Queen of the goblins, aka Deval's mom, winked at me.

I was part goblin. Maybe I could make the ground beneath me open up and swallow me whole. George tapped at our shared magical space as if to tell me that was a real option.

"To what do we owe the pleasure of your visit, mother, Pammy?" Deval gave a very formal nod to both women in turn. "Surely, it is not to analyze the dating styles of the modern times?"

"No, numb nuts, it's not to analyze the dating styles of the modern times," Pammy snapped back at him. "Bring me the remote."

No one was fazed by Pamela Goodwin, sheriff of the Arizona Witches, calling Deval Rouge, heir apparent of the southwest goblins, "numb nuts," so I didn't comment either.

"Remote?" I asked. Looking around confused at the request.

Pammy saw all of our confusion and marched over to the mantle, opening a small box that sat on top, and pulling out a remote. She pressed a button, and what I'd always assumed to be a fine oil painting split in half and slid back to reveal a sixty-inch television. I didn't have a chance to act surprised before Pammy turned on the local news channel. There was one of the teens we rescued talking ta a reporter.

"The witches came out of nowhere. Some of them were bad guys, and some of them seemed like the good guys. Two of these lady witches covered us up and protected us with their bodies. I think they did some magic, too. I don't remember much else, but we woke up in the park. But I know that we were there, man, there when it all exploded."

Pammy turned the TV off and turned to look at us.

"I'm out of town for less than two weeks, and y'all bring your war out in the open." Pammy pointed at Deval but notably did not do the same to Delmy. Then she turned to me. "You end up with a bunch of corpses in your pool. Have you even bothered to ward your yard yet?"

I meekly shook my head.

"I can't hear you."

"I got a little busy," I said this time.

"Yeah, a little busy is right. We're on the news. Where do we never want to be?"

She directed the question at me, but it was a universal truth for all of us, so we answered together.

"On the news."

"I've issued a challenge. Tomorrow we go to war. The victor will be decided by a single battle," Delmy informed the lot of us. The lot of us now included some of Delmy's people who had followed her to the library. I let them in at her request.

We'd moved some chairs and the six of us along with the goblin generals who'd arrived to join the party, had pulled the various wingback chairs from around the different nooks in the library, and we created a half circle around the fire. It had started to get a little warm with the extra bodies, but then I noticed Fred had called back some of my spies, and they interspersed about us, keeping a chill in the air that made the fire comforting rather than sweltering. I gestured for Fred to come closer.

"We're sure your comrades aren't buddy-buddy with Patrice?" I murmured to him but still caught several goblins look in my direction.

"No, Miss, your bargains are intact with them as long as you fulfill your promises within the thirty days we agreed upon."

I nodded.

"Is there a problem?" Delmy called out to me.

I squirmed in my chair a bit at being called out.

"No, just making sure that the spirits among us are allies."

The goblins all listened and nodded with a reverence they certainly hadn't had for me when I was a mere Soldier of Fortune. I reminded myself not to let it go to my head and gestured for Delmy to continue. That got a little bit of a look from her, but she then held up her hand.

"Griselda, bring me the map."

In the center of the chairs, we had placed a small side table. I wasn't sure what elaborate map she'd planned to place there, but I was a little surprised when Griselda handed her a brochure map I'd seen many times in my life. Delmy dramatically unfolded a map of the Arizona Renaissance Faire Grounds and placed it regally upon the table.

"We're going to war at the Ren Faire?" I asked before I could stop myself.

"It's the perfect place," she responded without hesitation. Acres upon acres of land deserted nine months out of the year, plus plenty of buildings in which to set a series of traps should our opponents dishonor the rules of war."

I raised my hand, this time, feeling odd to apparently be the only one with questions.

"Yes, Peg?" to her credit Delmy didn't sound annoyed with me.

"So, I guess I understand the location, but what are the rules? I've always been led to believe that wars are not won on individual battlefields. What determines the winner here? The lot of you aren't going to die unless there's a lot more beheading than I thought happened in a typical war —that and what if they're just really injured and scamper off. What makes this the final battle and not just an ongoing conflict where they break all the rules and really screw things up for the local witches? People see magic, and they think 'witch' because you guys aren't out in the open."

Delmy tilted her head and nodded at me. "I sometimes forget your lack of understanding of our established systems. Faxon has brought a mercenary army here to claim his kinghood. He has that right. We are a feudal society to a point. For the most part, we have fought his people in quiet ways, sure that he would eventually deplete his wealth, and alongside it, his power. It was an annoyance. Devastating at times.

Yesterday, he and his followers took things too far. Faxon has become obsessed with winning at all cost, and unbeknownst to him, his paid soldiers now, too, have a dog in this fight. They want you, Peg, and last night's fight showed me that they are willing to suffer great repercussions to collect you, perhaps even betraying Faxon."

"How do you know that?"

"I told her about the goblins trying to capture you," Griselda said.

Okay, that made sense.

"So, what we've been stuck with is that I had to call on the other goblin leaders across this country and other nations. They know that Faxon has gone too far, but again, our society rules by strength. So, we offer the challenge. It is binding, signed by all of the houses. This is a winner-takes-all battle from dusk until dawn. One of us will remain standing—either myself or Faxon.

If we both still live, then it will be down to numbers. I

will bring one hundred soldiers, and he will do the same. There will be a count at first light. If all goes according to plan, we will kill Faxon well before this time, but he is no great soldier and will hide among his people."

"What about Gregar? If Faxon dies, can he take up his father's banner?" I felt a little impressed with my lingo after binge watching one too many sword and dragon shows.

"He cannot, at least for this battle. I do not wish, per se, to kill my nephew, but he murdered his brother who was one of my loyal subjects and has conspired with his father against me. He will be executed either in battle or on another day. He is not our main focus."

"Do your hundred people include me?"

"If you are willing, I wish you on the battlefield. Pamela has also agreed to join us. Your witch sisters and brothers at arms will also be present at the battle to provide a magical shield across the property. If all goes according to plan, there should be minimal damage. There is a large parking area that is acre upon acre of empty desert. The road that runs along it goes to Florence and is rather desolate when the faire is not in town. Still, we must be cautious; we do not wish the sounds and flairs of our magic to be visible to outsiders. The witches' involvement has been approved along with the challenge. Only you and Pammy will be in the fight. The other witches will keep the cover through the night and into the morning during our clean up."

"I am willing," I said even though it felt like a rock dropped to the pit of my stomach.

Deval reached out and squeezed my knee reassuringly. Delmy actively ignored the small gesture.

"I know you are not trained in battle, Peg, although I know you are capable. Your true value, for lack of a better word is, bait. Should the insurgents pull any dirty tricks, we will use you to lure them into the faire grounds themselves. We have tricks of our own."

"So, we're not actually going to be in the faire grounds?" I asked gesturing toward the map on the table in front of me.

"Oh, we will be and have already begun to set up. Our hope is for a good clean battle, but if yesterday was any indication, we should not expect it. The rules of our wars are clear. We are to abide by them until we can't, meaning if our opponents want to play games, we will show them that if they can't handle the heat they should have stayed out of the desert."

Then the strategic planning began in earnest. Various traps were to be set up among the structures that the Ren Faire kept up all year long. There were the entry gates surrounded by two tower-like structures with a bridged balcony between them. While Delmy discussed this feature and the archers she planned to post there, Fred leaned toward me and whispered in my ear.

"I told you there would be wolves at the gate, Miss."

I looked to him and nodded, unsure if he was telling me he had a touch of clairvoyance, or if he just wanted to point out a coincidence with a dramatic flair. *Questions for later*.

The planning continued well past midnight with my role being described as "in the back" and "make yourself visible" and asking me how fast I could run. The answer was not fast. The solution to that was that I would have a horse brought for me. Bruce had volunteered one of his mounts. I didn't know what I feared more: the concept of my sprinting skills determining my fate or having to hang onto a saddle horn for dear life because my horseback riding experience consisted of the occasional trail ride with Bruce.

"She's bomb proof." Bruce used the lingo to describe an un-spookable horse. "She's a barrel horse, and she's fast, but I put the kiddos on her, so she won't give you any trouble."

"Even if weapons are going off around her?" I asked, uncertain that a "bombproof" horse would actually be bombproof.

"There will be no modern weapons. It is not our way, and their use would mean an automatic disqualification."

"Seriously?" I asked.

"When I said feudal rules, I meant it. Literal strength, Peg." Delmy literally flexed her bicep and pointed at it. It was a very impressive bicep.

"But you said they would try and do dishonest things. What if they literally bring a gun to a knife fight."

"Then they will have a bunch of pissed off witches zapping their asses with whatever dirty ass trick we can think of. My people did not sign up for bullets." Pammy had remained quiet throughout the planning but put in her two cents now.

"They will not." Delmy shut the conversation down. "They can pull a lot of dishonorable things, but automatic weapons would have all of goblinkind up in arms. Faxon wouldn't last a week on his throne. He knows that is not a minor faux pas he can get away with breaking."

Reassured, Pammy nodded and Delmy continued. "There were many places to hide and plot within the grounds. Stages, towers, a giant tank meant to hold mermaids, pavilions, kitchens, and of course the arena meant for jousts. I didn't ask Delmy, but I did lean toward Deval and whisper.

"Just want to confirm again, no one expects me to carry a lance, right?"

He just leaned in and laughed softly in my ear.

I took that as a "no."

Delmy spoke to and continued to plan with her people about aspects I would not be involved in, and I was embarrassed when Pammy caught me nodding off and announced to the group, "This one has an arbitration in the morning and needs to get home to bed." *It was like my mom had just told me I'd missed curfew.* My cheeks flooded with heat even as the other people around the room nodded in understanding.

"Arbitration? Tomorrow?" I asked Pammy. It was supposed to be on Monday.

"Yup, I called Yvette as soon as I hit the state border. She insisted on handling the arbitration still. I thought about fighting her on it, but I hit a section with no cell service, so the next time I talked to her was when I was pulling up here. She told me what you sent over. Looks like you're in the clear, kiddo, and I will be there with you. Should just be formalities."

I nodded, but it didn't feel real. How could something that had so disrupted my life, outing me to the world, end so easily? Pammy looked certain, but my stomach rolled into knots.

"Okay, sounds good. Are you meeting me there?"

"Nope, picking you up."

Great, another life threatening activity to add to my day tomorrow: driving with Pammy, being on trial for a murder and for the possibility of being stripped of my mantle, and end the day with an epic goblin battle where my role was "bait." So many things to look forward to.

I stood to leave and Deval and Delmy stood at the same time.

"Stay here, dear, I need a word with Peg."

Deval looked as if he was going to argue with his mother.

"Not to worry dear, this is not about her becoming my future-daughter-in-law, just a little magic talk."

Again, where was the hole that I could supposedly create in the ground to come and swallow me up?

Deval didn't argue; he just leaned down and gave me a kiss on my shell-shocked mouth before whispering in my ear, "courage."

I didn't know what to say to that, so I just pointed to the stairs indicating the way I was going.

Delmy nodded.

She followed behind me on the stairs.

She wouldn't push me down right? I didn't know why I was suddenly paranoid with the thought of having upset the queen.

"Relax, Peg, I like you with my son. This is about your pathways."

Relief flooded my system, and I let out a deep breath.

We didn't speak until we stood in front of one of my literal pathways: the door that stretched between the Library, my plane George, and my goblin safe.

"I heard what you did for my people, and I appreciate it."

There was a pause where a "but" usually went.

"But…"

And there it was.

"You must be careful of these powers. Opening these paths is an incredible gift, but it can thin the walls to your plane, which can leave you open to breaches. Your and my son's planes are connected. Maybe not physically yet, but in time. If this relationship kindles into the blaze as I suspect it will, you will be able to come and go freely among each other's realms. Not just when you call to one other. I understand that you do not need to supply wealth into your realm to fuel the power it brings you. Deval, however, does."

"So, what you're saying is don't go punching holes into my realm because I might be setting up Deval to get robbed?"

"I always knew you were a smart girl." Delmy reached out and grabbed me by both shoulders and pulled me in kissing me on both cheeks before pulling back to look at me. "To be clear, I am not saying never to do it. I am saying to reserve this gift for times that it is absolutely necessary. Last night was one of those times."

With that, she turned and headed back inside, leaving me to wander home alone.

16

The following morning, Pammy showed up at my house. I got in her old Crown Royal and she immediately shoved an iced coffee at me.

"My hero," I said before immediately downing half the concoction.

"Easy girl, we've got quite the day in front of us."

She seemed to take her own words to heart and for the first time that I could remember, she drove at reasonable speed and skipped the aggressive lane switching. We arrived at eight forty-five and given my recent familiarity with the Desert Princess found the appointed suite on time. Yvette Sarcona opened the door and greeted us both formally. The previous animosity I'd felt from her was gone.

We found our seats. Petunia and Adelaide had taken the same sofa that they had the last time; the absence of Carlita was noticeable, and I felt for the family. I had no idea what had led to her death, but Petunia looked distraught and a little green around the gills, no doubt from her libations the day before. I felt a little less upset about paying her bar tab.

"Ladies, we'll keep this short. New evidence has come to light, and I have made my decision."

"Wait, what about the evidence that I gathered?" Adelaide piped up.

"What is your new evidence?" Yvette asked.

"Well, uh, just that I found an entry in one of Aunt Alice's history books: it states for a fact that our family are the ones that created the Death Mantle. That should make it our property…" She trailed off at the end when the arbitrator didn't look particularly moved.

"That was never in doubt, young lady. The question was as to whether it was your right to keep it in the family. Pamela has given me list she'd compiled of every known mantle holder over the last two centuries. It's not complete, but you led me to believe that outsiders holding the mantle were a mere blip that could be explained by the peculiar transfer procedure for the magic.

Predicting one's death can be near impossible, so I wouldn't expect the Belgardes to continuously hold the power, but this list shows that your family has held it slightly fewer than fifty percent of the time. I cannot just ask this woman to risk her own death to appease some misplaced sense of ownership. I let my own family position cloud my judgment, but you two mislead me." Yvette stared at Adelaide almost daring her to argue.

Instead, the young woman sat there. Mouth wide open like a guppy before she finally snapped it shut. Her facial expression went from surprise to fury, but she continued to keep her mouth shut.

"When did you have time to gather a list?" I whispered to Pammy.

"Delmy did it when I asked her to; she's been around a

lot longer than either of us," she responded not bothering to whisper.

Adelaide shot her a glare and looked like she was about to speak again. Yvette once more held up a hand to silence her.

"It is bad enough that you would plead a false case to me and strategically place me here when this young woman's patron was out of town, but I now know the depths your family will go to in order to maintain the mantle." She turned her attention to Petunia who just stared straight ahead, glassy eyed. "I don't know what you thought that killing your own sister and framing this woman for her murder would gain you. I didn't try your case in the eighties. I was too young, but my father did."

"When I called him to speak of it, he confirmed the remarkable skill that your family had developed—trans-forming your hands for ill gains. It is obvious that you come from an incredibly gifted family, but you have thrown that away for foolish greed. The truly horrifying thing of this entire scenario is that your ploys might have worked had it not been for the intended scapegoat having a gentleman caller. You would have shamed me and my title by causing me to convict this young woman."

Petunia still had no response. She just sat there, offering no defense.

"Petunia Marie Belgarde, I sentence you to life imprisonment at the Trinity Correctional Facility."

Only then did Petunia respond. She leaned forward in her seat and let out a ragged sob, her head in her hands. "I would never hurt my sister."

"My father remembers a different relationship than the one you have presented to me. He remembered two bickering and adversarial women."

Adelaide rubbed her back, whispering to her aunt as

the woman sobbed, but offered no objection to her aunt's sentence.

It was hard to watch, and my gut clenched in empathy. I thought I would feel relief, or at least a satisfaction, but there was nothing harder than watching another person fall to such a low point. Even if she had murdered her sister, my heart ached for her, well not so much her but for the potential every person possessed and how easily circumstances and choices could destroy everything that person valued. I wouldn't make a good judge.

"Let's go," Pammy said quietly to me.

I half rose and half stumbled out of the chair, too caught up in the emotional currents in front of me.

"Do you need anything else from me?" Pammy asked.

"I have it from here," Yvette responded without looking back.

I saw her reach out and pull out a pair of handcuffs. The black metal of the heavy cuffs had symbols worked in copper throughout them. They should have been beautiful, but I took one look at them and sucked in my breath—a visceral reaction to the leeches. They were magical hand-cuffs that sucked out the magic, making any witch harmless.

I ran out of the room at the sight of them and didn't stop until I was halfway down the hallway. I wanted to lean against the wall and catch my breath, but I wanted to be away from that putrid magic even more. Pammy caught up with me and placed her hand on my shoulder.

"Breathe, Sug. You feel them more because you're part goblin. You can feel the metal."

Between the hand on the shoulder and the explanation to my strong reaction, I felt just a little bit better, but I walked to the doors at a breakneck speed and didn't take a full breath until we were outside. There I bent over, hands on knees, and dry heaved. I managed not to throw up the earlier latte, but just barely.

Two men in swimming attire walked by us as Pammy patted me on the back.

"Rough night?" One of them called out.

"Get bent," Pammy responded on my behalf.

Miraculously, they left without further comment.

"I just need some water."

"I've got water in the car, Sug. We have got to go."

I straightened, still feeling queasy, and managed to make it back to the car. Pammy blasted the AC and the cold air made me feel a little better. She didn't comment as we drove, and I stared out the window slowly finishing off the warm, metallic-tasting water from a water bottle that had been left in the sun.

I didn't say anything until she pulled in front of my house.

"Shouldn't we be heading to the battlegrounds to prepare?"

"Nope, I should be heading to Bump and Grind to talk with the other fortunes about our game plan. You should go in and take a load off in that plane of yours. You'll feel better and be ready for tonight. You've had a tough few months and a tougher couple of days. I'll text you when I'm on my way back to pick you up."

I didn't argue.

17

We arrived well before dusk, pulling off the 60 freeway into a field of dirt that would have been marked as a parking lot when the Arizona Renaissance Festival was in town. Now the entryway just looked like a dodgy side road. I didn't see anything but an empty dirt field at first, but then the veil parted, and a vast number of goblins came into view. The two armies stayed on their respective sides a good quarter of a mile from one another on the dirt field.

A lyrical hum filled the air. My people, the witches, already in place, were masking the battle stage from the view of any unwitting humans who passed by. I didn't envy them the night in front of them. Holding a shield that large would be exhausting, but the coward in me would have traded places with any of them even if it meant suffering from laryngitis from holding the song that worked the magic.

Pammy dropped me off with Delmy's people. They were evident since they wore the desert camo fatigues, while Faxon's people retained their all-black uniforms.

I'd dressed appropriately, not that I'd been sent a memo, but in analyzing what one wore to war, I'd found an old pair of heavy tan cargo pants left behind by a forgotten boyfriend, a brown shirt, and lace-up boots that were suitable for running or riding; my two party tricks for the evening. One of Delmy's people spotted me and immediately ushered me into their ranks from which Griselda emerged.

"You ready for this?" She asked striding toward me.

"I guess we'll find out," I said all the while wondering if they would think less of me for peeing my pants.

She studied my face. "It's good to be scared, but don't let it paralyze you."

"That's the plan." I tried to sound confident and failed spectacularly.

"I have some armor for you," she said and gestured to me to follow her into the crowd.

I didn't know what I'd been expecting, but the leather breastplate that was put over my head wasn't it. It was tight but still flexible. I did a few twists, feeling it move with my body. I didn't know what armor was supposed to feel like, so when it didn't pinch anything, I gave Griselda a thumbs up. I looked around and watched as the other goblins donned their own gear and noticed that several of them had helmets.

"Should I have one of those?" I pointed.

She shook her head. "We want you visible. Part of your protection is the idea that it has been made very clear that they don't want you dead."

"Cool, cool, but like should I be concerned about an arrow to the eye or something?" I knew I sounded like a moron as soon as I said it.

Griselda gave me a long look. "Yes, we should all be concerned about an arrow to the eye."

Right.

"Well, uh, where's my horse?"

Griselda held up her hand and snapped her fingers. "Ferdinand, bring the horse."

I didn't know much about horses, but this one was absolutely stunning, white and chestnut patterns splayed across her entire body. The paint mare had been outfitted with a western saddle and her own armor: worked leather covered her chest and sloped over her hindquarters. The goblin man led her forward and handed me the reins as if I knew what to do with them. I felt panicked until the horse leaned her velvety soft nose into my hand and let out a huff.

"Your friend brought her around this afternoon. Her name is Thunder," the goblin man said.

"Is he still here?" I asked a little too hopefully. I could use a Bruce hug and pep talk.

"We would not ask him to participate. He would need to ask his people, and it would have been huge ordeal to involve the shifters at this stage," Griselda told me. "He wanted me to let you know that her name is Thunder, don't pull on her mouth, and remember to use your legs. He did a blessing on the horse for luck in battle."

I was still trying to keep myself together, so I just nodded.

"You know how to mount, yes?" Griselda asked.

"Uh, yes?"

"If you have any trouble, ask one of us for a leg up."

I didn't really expect that to be practical in the middle of a battle, but I didn't say anything to contradict her.

"You will be at the back of the field. Stay off of the horse unless you need to flee. Stray arrows are more likely to hit you if you sit on horseback."

"Good to know. Anything else?" I managed to hide the tremble in my voice.

"Live through the night, and in the morning we will celebrate."

I couldn't think of anything to say and didn't need to because a low vibrating hum that harmonized with the witches' higher pitched song filled the air. The goblins around me began to stomp their feet to a beat, their earth magic making the ground tremble beneath me. Thunder let out a low nicker but didn't appear concerned.

The group parted, and Delmy strode down the path made for her. Her dark hair had been set in elaborate braids twisted along her scalp. She wore the tans and browns like her fighters, but her breastplate glowed with molten metal that twisted like a living being on her torso. She was mesmerizing, power and strength rolled off of her with every step she took. I almost missed Deval, who walked a foot behind her. Delmy gave me a nod as she passed me.

Deval reached out to me and grasped my hand brushing a kiss along my knuckles but continued his walk, flanking the queen. She went another ten feet before she stopped at the center of the crowd. A simple wooden box about two feet high was placed there and Deval lifted his mother upon it. She turned in a full circle surveying the crowd. The stomping stopped and the hum from the witches became an eerie howl in the quiet.

"A coward has returned with a bought army to try to rule us," she began, her voice deep and strong. "Do we let cowards rule?"

"No!" came from the crowd in a roar.

"The weak do not rule us!" She continued. "Their fumbling ways have endangered our very existence. Put our allies in danger. Killed our people. They have tried their tricks and will likely try them again this night. Be fierce, my friends. Be cunning. Be watchful. Live. We will not let them take our riches, our lands, and shame us in our own home. I will fight beside you, and we will return home. Home, to where I have copious amounts of alcohol." She winked then. She'd been serious up until that point, and the tension broke as everyone laughed around me.

"I will hold you to that!" Someone called out from the crowd.

"I wouldn't dare to disappoint," she responded not missing a beat. "Remember your comrades. Work together. Together we win: we live; we return to our people! To your stations!" She yelled this last bit, and I saw that the sun had just begun to fade behind the far off mountain ranges to the West. The soldiers moved in unison, all knowing their places. I stood rooted to the ground, numb, and then he was there.

Deval stood in front of me and took my face in his hands looking deeply into my eyes. His had gone molten, and I felt my own flaring in response.

"You are always the one telling me that you are capable of more than any of us could suspect. You have taken on the worst of your kind—the most ruthless of vampires, and you are the one who remains. Do not be hasty but be assured in your own strength. You have shown me that you can and will succeed."

My anxiety was still there. I would be stupid not to feel it, but the power of his confidence in me reminded me of my own well-earned pride. I nodded, my face still in his hands.

"I'm guessing you won't be hanging out with me tonight," I asked already knowing the answer.

"It would not be a true test of strength if the leaders are not on the front lines."

I laughed. "So, what does that say about putting me at the back?"

"It says that that tonight you serve a different purpose."

He kissed me then, hard and deep, and it ended much too soon.

"Fight well, live, I have some ideas about how I want to celebrate our victory." He gave me a smile that would set anyone's hair on fire and turned, walking into the crowd and on to the front lines.

"Woo wee, the look he just gave you. I think I'm having a hot flash." Pammy came and stood beside me, fanning herself with her hand.

She broke the tension that had hung in the air and had me doubling over with laughter for a moment before I straightened and looked at my guy.

"Is it weird that I kinda feel like I should have slapped him on the ass and said, "Go get 'em, tiger?"

Pammy gave an assessing look to Deval's departing figure.

"Sug, you should slap that ass any time the opportunity presents itself."

I looked over at her and saw that Pammy, too, had been given armor.

"Are you going to the front lines?" I asked.

"Hell, no, I'm sticking back here with you. We're not as fragile as they think, but I have no desire to come into contact with a broadsword. That is not our type of fight."

I looked around at the men, women, and others all lined up. They all carried heavy metal weapons.

The last rays of an Arizona sunset: pink, purple, and orange dipped behind the mountains. A piercing note from a horn sounded in the night while a magical flair lit the night sky, simultaneously exploding like a golden fire-cracker in the dusk sky. The sudden roar of battle was deafening as soldiers charged into the fight. The hair on my arms and the back of my neck stood up as their weapons began to glow in unison, crashing into one another, sending sparks into the air.

The roar died down, but new sounds emerged. Clashing metal, moving earth, screams and grunts as metal met flesh. I stood still in shock at the onslaught.

"They didn't ask us here to stand and look pretty," Pammy yelled at me breaking me from my stupor.

Actually, they had kind of asked me to do that, but I saw Pammy's hands begin to glow as she mumbled an incantation under her breath. She raised her hands, and her own magic lit up the sky with a deep purple as she sent knock-back spell after knock-back spell to the opposing fighters in the distance. Tripping them up as they went hand-to-hand with our people.

George pounded on the door in our shared magical realm asking to join in the fight. My magic flared to life combining all of the facets of my magic. I saw the green from my witch self, copper sparks from my goblin self, and finally the Death Mantle, a deep purple, all twined together. I'd meant to follow Pammy's lead and send a series of knock-back spells, but then I had another idea. My magic twined about itself like a rope. It whipped about haphazardly at first but steadied and reached out tasting at the soldiers in battle. The goblins from the southwest carried a unique signature in their bodies.

Everyone had a unique signature, but I could feel a pattern that let me recognize my people: salt, copper, clay, hematite, quartz, obsidian, turquoise. I'd handled all of these before, felt them around me without being aware, but it was never so obvious as when I felt the foreign goblins.

They didn't feel wrong, just not one with the desert. With that knowing, I slashed my magic through the air directing it like a whip, striking at the invaders.

Pammy and I stood side by side, and I lost all sense of time as the battle raged in front of me. Bodies of the wounded had fallen to the ground, and their uninjured brethren did their best to disengage and move their people out of further harm's way, so they wouldn't meet their final death. I started focusing my efforts on these people. Protecting the men and women who carried and dragged their friends out of immediate danger. They saw this and started moving the wounded to where we stood, leaving the wounded bodies in front of us.

I was tempted to stop and help the injured soldiers, but I couldn't disconnect from the magic. I was afraid I wouldn't be able to re-create the whip or the knowing of which soldiers were enemies in the dark if I stopped even for a moment, so, instead, I used my magic to shepherd the fallen to safety by blitzing any enemy who dared to follow.

I couldn't see Deval or Delmy until the hoard had thinned. After who knew how many hours, I saw them fighting back to back in the center of it all. Earth shot from the ground around them as they used both sword and their earth powers to subdue their opponents. Faxon was there as well, but he wasn't fighting. The weasel stood back, surrounded by guards and watched his sister and nephew fight for their lives.

"Cover the wounded, Pammy," an eerie sounding voice came from my mouth. My magic was running deeper than I thought, causing a magical vibration to alter it.

"You got it."

I extended my magic further than it had any right to go, and I felt it stretch to an almost painful distance. I let it strike, imagining it as a diamondback rattler lashing out at its prey. One after another, I knocked away Faxon's guards, leaving the man exposed and vulnerable for the first time. I couldn't see Delmy's face, but I saw her body language change and as quickly as that, she moved, leaving Deval behind as she moved to cut the head from the viper.

Faxon managed to meet her first swing and used his size to bear down on his smaller sister. She twisted away and ducked under the rebound of his sword; straightening quickly, she slashed her blade in a wide arch. I could see her pumping more magic into the sword as she swung, giving it the look of molten metal. Faxon's head left his body before I could blink.

The horn sounded immediately, and another flare lit up the sky, flashing against the boundary that the witches still held. Everything stopped at once, and it was startlingly quiet except for the witches' hum.

The quiet didn't last long. Delmy walked, undisturbed, to where her brother's head had landed, grabbed it by the hair and held it high. Her people went off with shouts, hollering, and began stomping the ground once more. I didn't realize I was still scanning the crowd, my magic looking for a target until Pammy put her hand on my arm.

"It's over, Sug. Dial it back."

My magic snapped back, and I found myself falling to my knees utterly and completely spent. I would have happily stayed on the ground if I didn't hear a man call out in a strong accent, managing to be heard above the crowd.

"Wolfe!" They appeared from the dark surrounding desert, dozens of fresh goblins that hadn't been in the battle.

Gregar stepped into the fray. I hadn't seen him in the battle, and now I understood why. He'd stayed back with the second wave.

"Kill Delmy!" He shrieked at the newcomers.

Delmy's people surrounded her in a protective stance, but no one made a move toward the Goblin Queen.

Another man stepped next to Gregar. He was older, grizzled, and it was immediately apparent he was in charge. He backhanded the younger goblin, knocking him down. "Fool," his voice carried across the field. "You have lost," he spat down at Gregar before looking up across the field. "Wolfe, seize our bounty!"

His eyes locked on mine, and they flashed silver.

Well, shit.

"That's your queue, Sug." Pammy grabbed me by the arm and dragged me up, turning me toward Thunder as the new soldiers rushed toward me.

"Protect her!" Delmy shouted and the battle began once more, but the mercenaries didn't want to stay in the fray. They had one purpose and that was apparently me. I scrambled frantically trying to gain the energy to get in the saddle. I began to panic when I felt a pair of hands at my waist. I'd begun to struggle, but I heard a familiar voice.

"It is Teddy. I am helping you."

I relaxed and let the man fling me into the saddle. I barely had time to grasp the reigns when Ted slapped Thunder's backside and sent us into a gallop. I gripped the horn with one hand, barely remembering how to navigate with the neck rein signals as I struggled to relax my body enough to flow into rhythm with the horse. We rushed under the entry bridge as we had talked about before, and I saw our archers stand up and take aim.

The path split then, and I managed to remember to turn right. I needed to get to the jousting arena, but first I needed to lead our enemies into the traps. We passed the buildings that housed shops and kitchens during the faire. Now they acted as hiding spots for our own fresh soldiers, and I saw them melt out of the shadows, weapons blazing. I shouldn't have looked back, but I did as I heard the screams from behind me. I couldn't stop myself. The enemy was moving faster than anyone had a right to on two legs, and there was a swarm of them. Some got caught up in the traps, but others were still definitely on my tail. I saw molten metal being thrown out of the balconies scalding them, but still they pursued me.

Thunder made a hard jolt to the left that nearly had me on my ass, but I managed to right myself, pulling on the saddle horn. The horse cried out when I did that and ran faster.

"I'm so sorry; I'm so sorry," I told her over and over again as I hung on for dear life. We flew past the Birds of Prey field. I blinked when I saw actual hawks and raptors emerge from the turret on the field.

Seriously? I thought to myself but was relieved to hear more screams behind me. I pictured the birds clawing at the mercenaries, but I didn't look back this time. We kept going, past the Queen's Kitchens and the various shops until I finally saw my destination: the jousting field. I passed under the arch into the arena and rode at a dead gallop to the far end before I finally managed to rein in Thunder. She stopped on a dime and did a rollback spinning quickly on her hindquarters to face the entrance. In the process, I fell to the front of the saddle, the horn punching me in the stomach, temporarily winding me.

Goblins fell into the arena, bloodied but still fighting. I reached for my magic, but it was only a flicker. George and I were both spent. It was a miracle I was still conscious. Through the fray, I saw the leader who had backhanded Gregar walk into the field. He ignored the battle around him and managed to slip through the fighters, making a beeline for me.

Oh, dear gods.

"Do you wish us to swarm him, Miss?"

This time I did fall out of the saddle. Fred's sudden appearance startling my already shaky self. I landed on the hot dirt face down, I tasted blood and dirt in my mouth. I managed to find the strength to push myself up. The man was ten feet from me and closing in fast, but I felt it then. The oppressive heat that surrounded me dropped twenty degrees in an instant, and I saw ghosts, more ghosts than I could count popped into existence.

"Get him," I answered Fred's question.

The enemy general had faltered when he felt the drop in temperature. He knew what I was, and I thought he might be trying to start the vibration to scatter them, but he wasn't fast enough. It was just like the encounter at Jolene's except on a much larger scale. They wrapped around him, creating a funnel that froze him in place. The ghosts were cackling in glee that was disturbing on a deep level, but I was the only one who could hear them. The goblin's steely grey hair lightened before my eyes to a feathery white. Then everything went black.

18

"It's bad form to miss your own celebration party." I heard Deval's voice through the fog of what felt like spider webs in my head.

"What party?" I managed to whisper. I'd attempted to open my eyes, but they felt too heavy to lift.

"The celebration, of course. The battle was fought and won. Faxon is dead."

"I saw that," I mumbled, eyes still closed.

"Gregar was also executed."

"I didn't see that."

"You have put the leader of Beast's Folly into a form of comatose delirium."

"That was the spirits," I whispered.

"There was tequila and whiskey by the barrel."

I finally managed to lift one eyelid. "You went to the party without me?" I asked. I didn't want to begrudge him a celebration, but my generation had major FOMO, fear of missing out, and I didn't want to hear about what I'd missed.

"Of course not." His lips brushed my forehead.

I sighed.

"My mother sends her regards."

"Cool, tell her I said 'hi' and that she should send me a barrel of tequila."

"It will be done," he responded without missing a beat.

"No, no, no, it was a joke. There can be too much of a good thing. Nobody needs a whole barrel." I didn't even want to think about the possible alcohol poisoning. I already felt terrible. I shut the one eye I'd managed to open. It was too hard to stay awake, let alone keep my eyes open. "What's wrong with me?"

"Nothing that won't heal in time. You've depleted yourself and somehow managed to put a serious strain on your plane. That and I would not say that horseback riding agrees with you. You are one very large bruise, madame."

"Tell me something I don't know. Is George going to be okay? Is Thunder okay?"

"The horse is fine, although Bruce advised me that I would be paying for an equine massage therapist for her. I think it is deserved. George, too, will recover, but it will take time, and in the meantime your mediation sessions in him will need to halt. Reach for him in your mind and reassure and comfort him, but he does not have the energy to heal you and himself."

My stomach twisted in guilt.

"I should have stopped earlier. I held the magic for too long."

"You helped protect dozens of my people. I'm not sure exactly what you did. I was a little busy, but I hadn't seen the likes of what you did before. When you are better; you can tell me all about it."

"Sure," I agreed. "Is Pammy okay?" I kept remembering things I needed to worry about.

"Of course she is. She was here earlier today to visit

you. She even brought you an iced latte on the off chance you'd be awake."

"Not now, I think I need to go back to sleep," I mumbled.

"You truly do not feel well. Rest now, and I will watch over you."

"And feed my cat."

"And feed your cat," he agreed as I drifted off.

I had no idea how long I'd slept but I woke up feeling as weak as a newborn kitten. Deval sat next to me in my bed. He was above the covers, fully clothed, but barefoot, one ankle crossed over the other, as he read a book.

"For the record, we're going to have that roll in the hay you promised me on the battlefield," I told him, "it's just not going to be today."

He closed the book and looked over at me and smiled. "I am a patient man."

"Good," I responded having exhausted my capacity for suggestive conversation. I was still bone-tired, but now I could hold my eyes open. I felt confident that I could make it to the bathroom on my own, which was good because my bladder was screaming at me.

Deval helped me stand even though I told him it wasn't necessary. He made me lean on him while I hobbled to the bathroom.

Sexy.

When I emerged, he helped me to my couch. If I was going to be an invalid, I was going to watch trash TV while I suffered. He had one of his people deliver Aliberto's to my home, and I wolfed and down a bean and cheese burrito that was twice as big as was necessary and set me up with a large water telling me that I needed H2O more than I needed Diet Pepsi. I knew he was right, but I was also feeling slightly contrary.

"Are you okay if I leave you for the afternoon?" He asked, a look of concern on his face.

"Honestly, yes. I'm not planning on popping in a step aerobics video, but I can make it from here to the bathroom or to my bed. Anything else I need, I can have delivered."

"The joys of the modern age."

"Exactly. Where are you headed off to?"

"I must meet with my people and do a walk through of the faire grounds to make sure we restored everything properly."

"And how would you know that?" I asked genuinely curious.

"I actually enjoy the faire and go regularly when it is in town."

I had not expected that, but I decided not to tease him.

"Do you wish me to have someone come stay with you. I'm sure they will appear soon enough on their own, but I could call Lola, Bruce, Pammy?"

"Nope. I want to sit here and do nothing." My introvert batteries were drained, but I didn't need to explain that.

"I will return this eve then."

I fell asleep on the couch not even five minutes after he left, and when I did eventually wake it was to water running in my backyard. That was sweet. Deval was filling up my pool for me, I thought. I stood up still a little unsteady, but the food and rest had done me good, and I made my way through my Arizona room to my backyard. Sure enough, the hose was in the pool. I wasn't sure why he thought I would want to float around in what was recently the watery grave of Carlita, but it was the thought that counted.

Maybe he'd bought me another new one? I wondered as I approached the pool to check it out.

"I wouldn't do that, Miss!" Fred called out to allowing me to spin in time to only be grazed by the shovel that Adelaide wielded. Pain erupted in my head, and I fell into the side of the pool. She didn't waste any time throwing the shovel aside and bending down grabbing me by my lower legs and hoisting me into it. The water was warm when it hit me, but the pool was only half full. I sunk like a rock hitting the plastic lining at the bottom before floundering to get my head above water.

Stars clouded my vision. Not a good sign, but I still managed to see the revolver she had pointed at me when I surfaced.

"A gun?" I asked for no other reason than it was odd to see a magic wielder carrying one.

"They'll think one of your human neighbors did you in," she explained in a very rational tone.

"Fair enough," I said shaking my head from side to side trying to clear it.

I saw Fred ease toward her.

"I can feel the ghost, Peg. Tell them all to back off. I can shoot you in the noggin before they get a chance to touch me."

"Why don't you then?" I probably shouldn't have asked that but my concussed brain wanted an explanation.

"Oh, I'm gonna, but I'm not an evil spirited woman. I thought you should know why."

I thought this kind of thing only happened in movies. I managed not to say that out loud. "So, get it off your chest."

"If you'd just taken the reaper, I wouldn't have had to

do any this. Do you have any idea what I've had to deal with over the years? My mom literally sold me to my bitch aunts. Did you know that they pretended to love me, but I heard them. I heard them!" Her voice had gotten high-pitched and slightly hysterical.

"Heard them say what?" I prodded all the while trying to figure out how to get myself out of this.

"They only wanted me, so they could make me carry the mantle. The mantle can make you crazy. They wanted all the power, but they weren't willing to have the repercussions. They would have used up my powers, selling my services, until the day I died."

"That's a dick move," I agreed. "So, why are you doing this now?"

She looked at me as though I was the crazy one. "I still want the power, stupid. I just don't want to be somebody's lap dog. They've kept me under their thumbs my whole life. I'm not going to trade my sanity for their benefit. I'm going to trade my sanity for my own benefit."

"Logical enough," I agreed, panicking because I didn't think there was much else to this story.

That was until I saw Lola open my back gate and peek her head through. For once in her life she hadn't called out "yoo-hoo" upon entering. *Thank the gods.*

"Why did Carlita need to die?" I prodded Adelaide as Lola made her way slowly across the yard.

"I was watching your house. I saw those goblin guys drop the dead guy in your pool. I was planning to just kill you if you wouldn't drink the reaper. The arbitrator acted like she was going to vote against you, but there was no precedent. She wouldn't have done it despite what my naive aunts thought. The bitch just wanted a high profile case and to feel powerful for a minute."

"Yvette?" I asked as Lola continued to tiptoe across my rather large yard like a cartoon character.

"Yes, her father was a very respected arbitrator. She's kind of the family fuck-up, if I'm being honest."

"Right, but again, why Carlita?"

"I needed to get rid of them eventually anyway, and the goblins dropping off the body gave me the idea. The aunties didn't know, but I have the ability to transform, too. I saw it in one of their spell books and made the potion. It was a piece of cake. Do you know those bitches never even asked if I could pull off the family party trick? So self-absorbed. You know, I'd been watching you for a while. I didn't think I needed to worry about you knocking boots with some random guy."

"You and me both, sister," I responded without thinking but didn't correct her on the "random" part.

"He is pretty hot." She looked as though she thought she was confiding some big secret to me.

The sisters really had sheltered her.

"So you kill one, frame me to take the fall, and it wasn't a big deal using Petunia as the scapegoat after your initial plan fell through since you were going to get rid of her eventually anyway?"

"Bingo," she said and her eyes hardened just slightly.

My time would have been up if Lola hadn't finally reached her destination. She bent down and grabbed the shovel Adelaide had set aside and swung. I'd seen her finger begin to tense just as the shovel made contact, the shot fired, ringing loudly through the air. The bullet went wide and my blow-up pool instantly began to deflate around me as Adelaide fell to the ground, knocked out cold.

Lola hefted her shovel in the air in victory. "Booyah!"

"Why didn't you just hit her with some magic from across the yard?" I asked in exasperation.

Lola lowered the shovel spade down and leaned against the handle. "You know I really hadn't thought of that," she said. "The shovel just made sense after all of the movies you've made me watch."

I just stared at her.

"Don't give me that look! I saved you for once! Booy-ah!" she called out again.

"That you did. We need to call Pammy."

EPILOGUE

Pammy had been called and arrived to haul Adelaide off to pay for her crimes and secure the release of Petunia. Not, however, before lecturing me once again about warding my yard and to stop buying blowup pools, "for the sake of all things holy."

A few weeks passed, and I woke one morning to the sound of large mechanical equipment and people hollering at each other. I wasn't worried about anyone being in my space because only close friends and family had been keyed to my brand-spanking-new wards, and I figured the city was doing something to the road, or that my neighbors were up to some home improvement. I covered my head with a pillow and let out a groan while the noise only got louder. And, then, I heard it: Deval's voice. It sounded like he was telling someone to "dig over there."

What in the gods' names was happening?

I sat up and moved my pillow, rubbing my eyes, trying to get them to adjust from the onslaught of sunshine coming in from my window. I looked down at myself, my pajamas didn't expose any of my bits and bobs. Perfect. I swung one leg over the bed and managed to bonk Cheddar, who sat on the floor next to the bed. He let out a growl and slashed at my leg. I moved quickly and only felt a hint of his claws.

"Cheddar, if you don't want me to step on you, maybe don't sit by the bed," I chastised him.

He looked up at me, a devious sparkle in his eyes and purred.

Just as I'd thought, he did it on purpose.

I made my way down my hallway and through my kitchen where I cautiously pushed aside the curtain over the window to see what was going on in my yard. So help me if there was another dead body, I was ready to just make a false confession, just so I could be carted off to prison where I might be able to get some decent sleep.

I didn't see a body, but I did see a hoe: a backhoe digging a hole where my inflatable pool had met its tragic demise. I let the curtain fall back and made it to my backyard through my Arizona room.

Deval stood near the small tractor and gestured broadly to the man who stood next to him, holding what looked like a set of plans.

"I don't think she would want a water slide," he told the man.

"What is going on here?" I approached the two men, leery of whatever devious plot Deval had come up with.

"Ah, Peg, sorry to wake you. This is the contractor for your new pool." Deval said that as if this wasn't strange at all.

"I don't remember budgeting for a new pool or hiring anyone for that matter, Deval," I said.

"I know you enjoy floating in the summer evenings, and your Wal-Mart purchases have been historically cursed. For my sanity, and your continued freedom from incarceration and the grave, I believe it's best that we install the real thing."

"You just want to see me in a bikini on a regular basis."

"I will not argue with that."

I grinned at him, and he smiled back.

"So, why don't you think I'd want a water slide?"

ABOUT THE AUTHOR

 Originally from Arizona, I'm currently residing in Chicago, having traded an oven for a freezer. I write Urban Fantasy because I like spooky things. I have a degree in English Literature from Arizona State University and the typical laundry list of jobs that goes with it. When I'm not working the day job or writing, I enjoy eating, reading, watching TV, pretending to be an elf (RPG), coding, and spoiling my cats.